ALSO BY HANIF KUREISHI

SCREENPLAYS AND PLAYS
My Beautiful Laundrette
Sammy and Rosie Get Laid
London Kills Me
My Son the Fanatic
Sleep with Me

FICTION
The Buddha of Suburbia
The Black Album
Love in a Blue Time
Intimacy
Midnight All Day
Gabriel's Gift

NONFICTION
The Faber Book of Pop (edited with Jon Savage)
Dreaming and Scheming

THE BODY

a novel

HANIF KUREISHI

SCRIBNER

NEW YORK LONDON TORONTO SYDNEY

SCRIBNER
1230 Avenue of the Americas
New York, NY 10020

First Scribner edition 2004
Originally published in Great Britain in 2002 by Faber and Faber Limited

SCRIBNER and design are trademarks of
Macmillan Library Reference USA, Inc., used under license
by Simon & Schuster, the publisher of this work.

For information about special discounts for bulk purchases,
please contact Simon & Schuster Special Sales:
1-800-456-6798 or business@simonandschuster.com

Designed by Kyoko Watanabe

Text set in Stempel Garamond

Manufactured in the United States of America

1   3   5   7   9   10   8   6   4   2

Library of Congress Cataloging-in-Publication Data
Kureishi, Hanif.
The body : a novel / Hanif Kureishi.—1st Scribner ed.
p.   cm.
I. Title.
PR6061.U68B63 2004
823'.914—dc22   2003063309

ISBN 0-7432-4904-6

THE BODY

1

HE SAID, "Listen: you say you can't hear well and your back hurts. Your body won't stop reminding you of your ailing existence. Would you like to do something about it?"

"This half-dead old carcass?" I said. "Sure. What?"

"How about trading it in and getting something new?"

It was an invitation I couldn't say no to, or yes, for that matter. There was certainly nothing simple or straightforward about it. When I had heard the man's proposal, although I wanted to dismiss it as madness, I couldn't stop considering it. All that night I was excited by an idea that was—and had been for a while, now I was forced to confront it—inevitable.

This "adventure" started with a party I didn't want to go to.

Though the late 1950s and early 1960s were supposed to be my heyday, I don't like the assault of loud music, and I have come to appreciate silence in its many varieties. I am not crazy about half-raw barbecued food either.

Want to hear about my health? I don't feel particularly ill, but I am in my mid-sixties; my bed is my boat across these final years. My knees and back give me a lot of pain. I have hemorrhoids, an ulcer, and cataracts. When I eat, it's not unusual for me to spit out bits of tooth as I go. My ears seem to lose focus as the day goes on and people have to yell into me. I don't go to parties because I don't like to stand up. If I sit down, it makes it difficult for others to speak to me. Not that I am always interested in what they have to say; and if I am bored, I don't want to hang around, which might make me seem abrupt or arrogant.

I have friends in worse shape. If you're lucky, you'll be hearing about them. I do like to drink, but I can do that at home. Fortunately, I'm a cheap drunk. A few glasses and I can understand Lacan.

My wife, Margot, has been a counselor for five years, training now to be a therapist. She listens to people for a living, in a room in the house. We have been fortunate; each of us has always envied the other's profession. She has wanted to make from within; I need to hear from without.

Our children have left home, the girl training to be a doctor and the boy working as a film editor. I guess my life has had a happy ending. When my wife, Margot, walks into a room, I want to tell her what I've been thinking, some of which I know she will attend to. Margot, though, enjoys claiming that men start to get particularly bad-tempered, pompous, and demanding in late middle age. According to her, we stop thinking that politeness matters; we forget that other people are more important than ourselves. After that, it gets worse.

I'd agree that I'm not a man who has reached some kind of Buddhist plateau. I might have some virtues, such as compassion and occasional kindness; unlike several of my friends, I've never stopped being interested in others, or in culture and politics—in the general traffic of mankind. I have wanted to be a good enough father. Despite their necessary hatred of me at times, I enjoyed the kids and liked their company. So far, I can say I've been a tolerable husband overall. Margot claims I have always written for fame, money, and women's affection. I would have to add that I love what I do, too, and it continues to fascinate me. Through my work I think about the world, about what matters to me and to others.

Beside my numerous contradictions—I am, I have been told, at least three different people—I am unstable, too, lost in myself, envious, and constantly in need of reassurance. My wife says that I have crazinesses, bewildering moods and "internal disappearances" I am not even aware of. I can go into the shower as one man and emerge as another, worse, one. My pupils enlarge, I move around obsessively, I yell and stamp my feet. A few words of criticism and I can bear a grudge for three days at a time, convinced she is plotting against me. None of this has diminished, despite years of self-analysis, therapy, and "writing as healing," as some of my students used to call the attempt to make art. Nothing has cured me of myself, of the self I cling to. If you asked me, I would probably say that my problems are myself; my life is my dilemmas. I'd better enjoy them, then.

I wouldn't have considered attending this party if Margot hadn't gone out to dinner with a group of women friends, and if I hadn't envied what I saw as the intimacy and urgency of their conversation, their pleasure in one another. Men can't be so direct, it seems to me.

But if I stay in alone now, after an hour I am walking about picking things up, putting them down, and then searching everywhere for them. I no longer believe or hope that book knowledge will satisfy or even entertain me, and if I watch TV for too long I begin to feel hollow. How out of the world I already believe myself to be! I am no longer familiar with the pop stars, actors, or serials on TV. I'm never certain who the pornographic boy and girl bodies belong to. It is like trying to take part in a conversation of which I can only grasp a fraction. As for the politicians, I can barely make out which side they are on. My age, education, and experience seem to be no advantage. I imagine that to participate in the world with curiosity and pleasure, to see the point of what is going on, you have to be young and uninformed. Do I want to participate?

On this particular evening, with some semi-senile vacillation and nothing better to do, I showered, put on a white shirt, opened the front door, and trotted out. It was the height of summer and the streets were baking. Although I have lived in London since I was a student, when I open my front door today I am still excited by the thought of what I might see or hear, and by who I might run into and be made to think about. London seems no longer part of Britain — in my view, a dreary, narrow place full of fields, boarded-up shops, and cities trying to imitate London — but has developed into a semi-independent city-state, like New York, and has begun to come to terms with the importance of gratification. On the other hand, I had been discussing with Margot the fact that it was impossible to get to the end of the street without people stopping you to ask for money. Normally, I looked so shambolic myself the beggars lost hope even as they held out their hands.

It was a theater party, given by a friend, a director who also teaches. Some of her drama school pupils would be there, as well as the usual crowd, my friends and acquaintances, those who were still actively alive, not in hospital or away for the summer.

As my doctor had instructed me to take exercise, and still hoping I had the energy of a young man, I decided to walk from west London to the party. After about forty-five minutes I was breathless and feeble. There were no taxis around and I felt stranded on the dusty, mostly deserted streets. I wanted to sit down in a shaded park, but doubted whether I'd be able to get up again, and there was no one to help me. Many of the boozers I'd have dropped into for a pint of bitter and a read of the evening paper, full of local semi-derelicts escaping their families—alcoholics, they'd be called, now everyone has been pathologized—had become bars, bursting with hyperactive young people. I wouldn't have attempted to get past the huge doormen. At times, London appeared to be a city occupied by cameras and security people; you couldn't go through a door without being strip-searched or having your shoes and pockets examined, and all for your own good, though it seemed neither safer nor more dangerous than before. There was no possibility of engaging in those awful pub conversations with wretched strangers which connected you to the impressive singularity of other people's lives. The elderly seem to have been swept from the streets; the young appear to have wires coming out of their heads, supplying either music, voices on the phone, or the electricity that makes them move.

Yet I've always walked around London in the afternoons and evenings. These are relatively long distances, and I look at shops, obscure theaters, and strange museums, otherwise my body feels clogged up after a morning's desk work.

The party was held not in my friend's flat but in her rich brother's place, which turned out to be one of those five-floor, wide stucco houses near the zoo.

When at last I got to the door, a handful of kids in their twenties turned up at the same time.

"It's you," said one, staring. "We're doing you. You're on the syllabus."

"I hope I'm not causing you too much discomfort," I replied.

"We wondered if you might tell us what you were trying to do with—"

"I wish I could remember," I said. "Sorry."

"We heard you were sour and cynical," murmured another, adding, "and you don't look anything like your picture on the back of your books."

My friend whose party it was came to the door, took my arm, and led me through the house. Perhaps she thought I might run away. The truth is, these parties make me as anxious now as they did when I was twenty-five. What's worse is knowing that these terrors, destructive of one's pleasures as they are, are not only generated by one's own mind but are still inexplicable. As you age, the source of your convolutedly self-stymieing behavior seems almost beyond reach in the past; why, now, would you want to untangle it?

"Don't you just hate the young beautiful ones with their vanity and sentences beginning with the words 'when I left Oxford' or 'RADA'?" she said, getting me a drink. "But they're a necessity at any good party. A necessity anywhere anyone fancies a fuck, wouldn't you say?"

"Not that they'd want either of us too close to them," I said.

"Oh, I don't know," she said.

She took me out into the garden, where most people had gathered. It was surprisingly large, with both open and wooded areas, and I couldn't see the limits of it. Parts were lit by lanterns hung from trees; other areas were invitingly dark. There was a jazz combo, food, animated conversation, and everyone in minimal summer clothing.

I had fetched some food and a drink and was looking for a place to sit when my friend approached me again.

"Adam," she said. "Now, don't make a fuss, dear."

"What is it?"

My heart always sinks when I hear the words "there's someone who wants to meet you."

"Who is it?"

I sighed inwardly, and, no doubt, outwardly, when it turned out to be a young man at drama school, a tyro actor. He was standing behind her.

"Would you mind if I sat with you for a bit?" he said. He was going to ask me for a job, I knew it. "Don't worry, I don't want work."

I laughed. "Let's find a bench."

I wouldn't be curmudgeonly on such a delightful evening. Why shouldn't I listen to an actor? My life has been spent with those who transform themselves in the dark and make a living by calculating the effect they have on others.

My friend, seeing we were okay, left us.

I said, "I can't stand up for long."

"May I ask why?"

"A back problem. Only age, in other words."

He smiled and pointed. "There's a nice spot over there."

We walked through the garden to a bench surrounded by bushes where we could look out on the rest of the party.

"Ralph," he said. I put down my food and we shook hands. He was a beautiful young man, tall, handsome, and confident, without seeming immodest. "I know who you are. Before we talk, let me get us more champagne."

Whether it was the influence of Ralph, or the luminous, almost supernatural quality that the night seemed to have, I couldn't help noticing how well groomed everyone seemed, particularly the pierced, tattooed young men, as decorated as a jeweler's window, with their hair dyed in contrasting colors. Apart from the gym, these boys must have kept fit twisting and untwisting numerous jars, tubs, and bottles. They dressed to show off their bodies rather than their clothes.

One of the pleasures of being a man has been that of watching women dress and undress, paint and unpaint. When it comes to their bodies, women believe they're wearing the inside on the outside. However, the scale of the upkeep, the shop scouring and forethought, the possibilities of judgment, criticism, and sartorial inaccuracy as, in contrast, the man splashes water on his face and steps without fear into whatever he can find at the end of the bed and then out into the street, have never been enviable to me.

When Ralph returned and I busied myself eating and looking, he praised my work with enthusiasm and, more important, with extensive knowledge, even of its obscurer aspects. He'd seen the films I'd written and many productions of my numerous plays. He'd read my essays, reviews, and recently published memoirs, *Too Late*. (What a dismal business that final addition and subtraction had been, like writing an interminable will, and nothing to be done about any of it, except to turn and torture it in the hope of a more favorable outlook.) He knew my work well; it seemed to have meant a lot to him. Praise can be a trial; I endured it.

I was about to go to the trouble of standing up to fetch more food when Ralph mentioned an actor who'd played a small part in one of my plays in the early 1970s, and had died of leukemia soon after.

"Extraordinary actor," he said. "With a melancholy we all identified with."

"He was a good friend," I said. "But you wouldn't remember his performance."

"But I do."

"How old were you, four?"

"I was right there. In the stalls. I always had the best seats."

I studied his face as best I could in the available light. There was no doubt that he was in his early twenties.

"You must be mistaken," I said. "Is it what you heard? I've been spending time with a friend, someone I consider Britain's finest postwar director. Where is his work now? There can be no record of how it felt to watch a particular production. Even a film of it will yield no idea of the atmosphere, the size, the feeling of the work. Mind you," I added, "there are plenty of directors who'd admit that that was a mercy."

He interrupted. "I was there, and I wasn't a kid. Adam, do you have a little more time?"

I looked about, recognizing many familiar faces, some as wrinkled as old penises. I'd worked and argued with some of these people for more than thirty years. These days, when we met it was less an excited human exchange than a litany of decline; no one would put on our work, and if they did it wasn't sufficiently praised. Such bitterness, more than we were entitled to, was enervating. Or we would talk of grandchildren, hospitals, funerals and memorial services, saying how much we missed so-and-so, wondering, all the while, who would be next, when it would be our turn.

"Okay," I said. "Why would I be in a hurry? I was only thinking recently that after a certain age one always seems to be about to go to bed. But it's a relief to be done with success. I can lie down with the electric blanket on, listening to opera and reading badly. What a luxury reading badly can be, or doing anything badly for that matter."

Two young women had stationed themselves out of earshot, but close enough to observe us, turning occasionally to glance and giggle in our direction. I knew that the face out of which I looked was of no fascination to them.

He leaned toward me. "It's time I explained myself. Let's say . . . once there was a young man, not the first, who felt like Hamlet. As baffled, as mad and mentally chaotic, and as ruined by his parents. Still, he pulled himself together and became successful, by which I mean he made money doing something necessary but stupid. Manufacturing toilet rolls, say, or a new kind of tinned soup. He married, and brought up his children.

"In his middle age, as sometimes happens, he felt able to fall in love at last. In his case it was with the theater. He bought a flat in the West End so he could walk to the theater every night. He did this for years, but though he loved the gilt, the plush seats, the ice creams, the post-show discussions in expensive restaurants, it didn't satisfy him. He had begun to realize that he wanted to be an actor, to stand electrified before a large crowd every night. How could anything else fulfill him?

"But he was too old. He couldn't possibly go to drama school without feeling ridiculous. He was destined to be one of those unlucky people who realize too late what they want to do. A vocation is, after all, the backbone of a life.

"At the same time," he went on, "something terrible was happening. His wife, with whom he had been in love, suffered from a degenerative illness that destroyed her body but left her mind unharmed. She was, as she described it, a healthy driver in a car that wouldn't respond, that was deteriorating and would crash, killing her. She said that all she needed was a new body. They tried many treatments in several countries, but in the end she was begging for death. In fact, she asked her husband to take her life. He did not do this, but was considering it when she saved him the trouble."

"I'm sorry," I said.

"These days, dying can be a nightmare. People hang on for years, long after they've got anything to talk about."

He went on, "The man, who had been looking after his wife for ten years, retired and went on a trip to recuperate. However, he didn't feel that he had long to live. He was exhausted, old and impotent. He was preparing for death too.

"One day, in South America, where he knew other wealthy but somewhat dreary people, he heard a fantastic story from a young man he trusted, a doctor who, like him, was interested in the theater, in culture. Together—can you imagine?—they put on an amateur production of *Endgame*. This doctor was moved by the old man's wish for something unattainable. He confided in him, saying that an amazing thing was taking place. Certain old, rich men and women were having their living brains removed and transplanted into the bodies of the young dead."

Ralph became quiet here, as if he needed to know my reaction before he could continue.

I said, "It seems logical that technology and medical capability only need to catch up with the human imagination or will. I know nothing about science, but isn't this usually the way?"

Ralph went on, "These people might not exactly live forever, but they would become young again. They could be twenty-year-olds if they wanted. They could live the lives they believed they'd missed out on. They could do what everybody dreams of, have a second chance."

I murmured, "After a bit you realize there's only one invaluable commodity. Not gold or love, but time."

"Who hasn't asked: Why can't I be someone else? Who, really, wouldn't want to live again, given the chance?"

"I'm not convinced of that," I said. "Please continue. Were there people you met who had done this?"

"Yes."

"What were they like?"

"Make up your own mind." I turned to him again. "Go on," he said. "Have a good stare." He leaned into the light in order to let me see him. "Touch me if you want."

"It's all right," I said, prissily, after stroking his cheek, which felt like the flesh of any other young man. "Go on."

"I have followed your life from the beginning, in parallel to my own. I've spotted you in restaurants, even asked for your autograph. You have spoken my thoughts. My audition speech at drama school was a piece by you. Adam, I am older than you."

"This conversation is difficult to believe," I said. "Still, I always enjoyed fairy stories."

He continued, "As I told you, I had made money but my time was running out. You know better than me, an actor walks into a room and immediately you see—it's all you see—he's too old for the part. Yet one's store of desire doesn't diminish with age, with many it increases; the means to fulfill it become weakened. I didn't want a trim stomach, woven hair, or less baggy eyes, or any of those . . . trivial repairs." Here he laughed. It was the first time he hadn't seemed earnest. "What I wanted was another twenty years, at least, of health and youth. I had the operation."

"You had your brain removed . . . to become a younger man?"

"What I am saying sounds deranged. It is unbelievable."

"Let us pretend, for the sake of this enjoyable fantasy, that it really is true. How does it work?"

He said the procedure was terrifying, but physically not as awful as open-heart surgery, which we'd both had. When you come round from the anesthetic in this case, you feel fit and optimistic. "Ready to jump and run," as he put it. The operation wasn't exactly common yet. There were only a handful of surgeons who could do it. The procedure had been done hundreds of times, perhaps a thousand, he didn't know the exact figure, in the last five years. But it was still, as far as he knew, a secret. Now was the time to have it, at the beginning, before there was a rush; when it was still in everyone's interest to keep the secret.

He went on to say that there were certain people who he

believed needed more time on earth, for whom the benefit to mankind could be immense. To this I replied that although I didn't know him, it was his mildness that struck me. He didn't seem the type to lead some kind of master race. He wasn't Stalin, Pol Pot, or even Mother Teresa returning for another fifty years.

"That's right," he said. "Needless to say, I don't include myself in this. I had children and I worked hard. I needed another life in order to catch up on my sleep. If I'm back, it's for the crack!"

I asked, "If you really were one of these women or men, what would you want to do with your new time?"

"For years, all I've wanted is to play Hamlet. Not as a seventy-year-old but as a kid. That is what I'm going to do," he said. "At drama school, first. It's already been cast and I've got the part. I've known the lines for years. In my various factories, I'd walk about, speaking the verse, to keep sane."

"I hope you don't mind me pointing this out, but what's wrong with Lear or Prospero?"

"I will approach those pinnacles eventually. Adam, I can do anything now, anything!"

I said, "Is that what you are intending to do after you've played Hamlet?"

"I will continue as an actor, which I love. Adam, I have money, experience, health, and some intelligence. I've got the friends I want. The young people at the school, they're full of enthusiasm and ardor. Something you wrote influenced me. You said that unlike films, plays don't take place in the past. The fear, anxiety, and skill of the actors is happening now, in front of you. If performing is risky, we identify with the possibility of grandeur and disaster. I want that. I can tell you that what has happened to me is an innovation in the history of humankind. How about joining me?"

I was giggling. "I'm no saint, only a scribbler with an interest, sometimes, in how people use one another. I don't feel entitled to another go at life on the basis of my 'nobility.'"

"You're creative, contrary, and articulate," he said. "And, in my opinion, you've only just started to develop as an artist."

"Jesus, and I thought I'd had my say."

"You deserve to evolve. Meet me tomorrow morning." As he picked up his plate and glass from the floor, the two observing women, who had not lost patience, began to flutter. "We'll take it further then."

He touched me on the arm, named a place, and got up.

"What's the rush?" I said. "Can't we meet in a few days?"

"There is the security aspect," he said. "But I also believe the best decisions are taken immediately."

"I believe that too," I said. "But I don't know about this."

"Dream on it," he said. "You've heard enough for one evening. It would be too much for anyone to take in. See you tomorrow. It's getting late. I really want to dance. I can dance all night, without stimulants."

He pressed my hand, looked into my eyes as if we already had an understanding, and walked away.

The conversation had ended abruptly but not impolitely. Perhaps he had said all there was to say for the moment. He had certainly left me wanting to know more. Hadn't I, like everyone else, often thought of how I'd live had I known all that I know now? But wasn't it a ridiculous idea? If anything made life and feeling possible, it was transience.

I watched Ralph join a group of drama students, his "contemporaries." Like him, presumably, but unlike me, they didn't think of their own death every day.

I got up and briefly talked to my friends—the old fucks with watery eyes; some of them quite shrunken, their best work long done—finished my drink, and said goodbye to the host.

At the door, when I looked back, Ralph was dancing with a group of young people among whom were the two women who'd been watching him. Walking through the house, I saw the kids I'd met at the front door sitting at a long table drinking, playing with one another's hair. I was sure I could hear someone saying they preferred the book to the film, or was it the film to the book? Suddenly, I longed for a new world, one in which no one compared the book to the film, or vice versa. Ever.

In order to think, I walked home, but this time I didn't feel tired. As I went I was aware of groups of young men and women hanging around the streets. The boys, in long coats and hoods that concealed most of their faces, made me think of figures from *The Seventh Seal*. They made me recall my best friend's painful death, two months before.

"It won't be the same without me around," he had said. We had known each other since university. He was a bad alcoholic and fuckup. "Look at your life and all you've done. I've wasted my life."

"I don't know what waste means."

"Oh, I know what it is now," he had said. "The inability to take pleasure in oneself or others. Cheerio."

The chess pieces of my life were being removed one by one.

My friend's death had taken me by surprise; I had believed he would never give up his suffering. The end of my life was approaching too; there was a lot I was already unable to do, soon there would be more. I'd been alive a long time but my life, like most lives, seemed to have happened too quickly, when I was not ready.

The shouts of the street kids, their incomprehensibly hip vocabulary and threatening presence, reminded me of how much the needs of the young terrify the old. Maybe it would be interesting to know what they felt. I'm sure they would be willing to talk. But there was no way, until now, that I could actually have "had" their feelings.

At home, I looked at myself in the mirror. Margot had said that with my rotund stomach, veiny, spindly legs, and left-leaning posture I was beginning to resemble my father just before his death. Did that matter? What did I think a younger body would bring me? More love? Even I knew that that wasn't what I required as much as the ability to love more.

I waited up for my wife, watched her undress, and followed her instruction to sit in the bathroom as she bathed by candle-light, attending to her account of the day and—the highlight for me—who had annoyed her the most. She and I also liked to discuss our chocolate indulgences and bodies: which part of which of us, for example, seemed full of ice cream and was expanding. Various diets and possible types of exercise were always popular between us. She liked to accuse me of not being "toned," of being, in fact, "mush," but threatened murder and suicide if I mentioned any of her body parts without reverence. As I looked at her with her hair up, wearing a dressing gown and examining and cleaning her face in the mirror, I wondered how many more such ordinary nights we would have together.

A few minutes after getting into bed, she was slipping into sleep. I resented her ability to drop off. Although sleeping had come to seem more luxurious, I hadn't got any better at it. I guess children and older adults fear the separation from consciousness, as though it'll never return. If anyone asked me, I said that consciousness was the thing I liked most about life. But who doesn't need a rest from it now and again?

Lying beside Margot, chatting and sleeping, was exceptional every night. To be well married you have to have a penchant for the intricacies of intimacy and larval change: to be interested, for instance, in people dreaming together. If the personality is a spider's web, you will want to know every thread. Otherwise, after forty, when the color begins to drain from the world, it's either retirement or reinvention. Pleasures no longer come to you, but there are pickings to be had if you can learn to scavenge for them.

Later, unusually—it had been a long time—she woke me up to make love, which I did happily, telling her that I'd always loved her, and reminiscing, as we often did, about how we met and got together. These were our favorite stories, always the same and also slightly different so that I listened out for a new feeling or aspect.

For the rest of the night I was awake, walking about the house, wondering.

2

_____

THE FOLLOWING morning there was no question of not meeting Ralph at the coffee shop he'd suggested. At the same time I didn't believe he'd show up; perhaps that was my wish. He had made me think so hard, the scope of my everyday life seemed so mundane and I had become so excited about this possible adventure and future that I was already beginning to feel afraid.

He arrived on a bicycle, wearing few clothes, and told me he'd stayed up late dancing, woken up early, exercised, and studied a "dramatic text" before coming here. It was common, he said, that people living a "second" life, like people on a second marriage, took what they did more seriously. Each moment seemed even more precious. There was no doubt he looked fit, well, and ready to be interested in things.

I found myself studying his face. How should I put it? If the body is a picture of the mind, his body was like a map of a place that didn't exist. What I wanted was to see his original face, before he was reborn. Otherwise it was like speaking on the phone to someone you'd never met, trying to guess what they were really like.

But it was me, not him, we were there for, and he was businesslike, as I guessed he must have been in his former life. He went through everything as though reading from a clipboard in his mind. After two hours we shook hands, and I returned home.

Margot and I always talked and bickered over lunch together, soup and bread, or salad and sandwiches, before our afternoon nap on separate sofas. Today, I had to tell her I was going away.

Earlier in the year Margot had gone to Australia for two months to visit friends and travel. We needed each other, Margot and I, but we didn't want to turn our marriage into more of an enclosure than necessary. We had agreed that I, too, could go on "walkabout" if I wanted to. (Apparently, "walkabout" was called "the dreaming" by some Aboriginals.) I told her I wanted to leave in three days' time. I asked for "a six-month sabbatical." As well as being upset by the suddenness of my decision, she was shocked and hurt by the length of time I required. She and I are always pleased to part, but then, after a few days, we need to share our complaints. I guess that was how we knew our marriage was still alive. Yet she knew that when I make up my mind, I enter a tunnel of determination, for fear that vacillation is never far away.

She said, "Without you here to talk about yourself in bed, how will I go to sleep?"

"At least I am some use, then."

She acquiesced because she was kind. She didn't believe I'd last six months. In a few weeks I'd be bored and tired. How could anyone be as interested in my ailments as her?

It took me less time than I would have hoped to settle myaffairs before the "trip." I had a circle of male friends who came to the house once a fortnight to drink, watch football, and discuss the miseries of our work. Margot would inform them I was going walkabout and we would reconvene on my return. I made the necessary financial arrangements through my lawyer, and followed the other preparations Ralph had insisted on.

When Ralph and I met up again he took one look at me and said, "You're my first initiate. I'm delighted that you're doing this. You live your life trying to find out how to live a life, and then it ends. I don't think I could have picked a better person."

"Initiate?"

"I've been waiting for the right person to follow me down this path, and it's someone as distinguished as you!"

"I need to see what this will bring me," I murmured, mostly to myself.

"The face you have must have brought you plenty," he said. "Didn't you see those girls watching you at the party? They asked me later if you were really you."

"They did?"

"Now—ready?"

He was already walking to his car. I followed. Ralph was so solicitous and optimistic, I felt as comfortable as anyone could in the circumstances. Then I began to look forward to "the change" and fantasized about all that I would do in my new skin.

By now we'd arrived at the "hospital," a run-down warehouse on a bleak, windblown industrial estate outside London (he had already explained that "things would not be as they seemed"). I noticed from the size of the fence and the number of black-uniformed men that security was tight. Ralph and I showed our passports at the door. We were both searched.

Inside, the place did resemble a small, expensive private hospital. The walls, sofas, and pictures were pastel-colored and the building seemed almost silent, as if it had monumental walls. There were no patients moving about, no visitors with flowers, books, and fruit, only the occasional doctor and nurse. When I did glimpse, at the far end of a corridor, a withered old woman in a pink flannel nightgown being pushed in a wheelchair by an orderly, Ralph and I were rapidly ushered into a side office.

Immediately, the surgeon came into the room, a man in his mid-thirties who seemed so serene I could only wonder what kind of yoga or therapy he had had, and for how long.

His assistant ensured the paperwork was rapidly taken care of, and I wrote a check. It was for a considerable amount, money that would otherwise have gone to my children. I hoped scarcity would make them inventive and vital. My wife was already provided for. What was bothering me? I couldn't stop suspecting that this was a confidence trick, that I'd been made a fool of in my most vulnerable areas: my vanity and fear of decline and death. But if it was a hoax, it was a labored one, and I would have parted with money to hear about it.

The surgeon said, "We are delighted to have an artist of your caliber join us."

"Thank you."

"Have you done anything I might have heard of?"

"I doubt it."

"I think my wife saw one of your plays. She loves comedy and now has the leisure to enjoy herself. Ralph has told me that it's a short-term body rental you require, initially? The six-months minimum—is that correct?"

"That is correct," I said. "After six months I'll be happy to return to myself again."

"I have to warn you, not everyone wants to go back."

"I will. I am fascinated by this experiment and want to be involved, but I'm not particularly unhappy with my life."

"You might be unhappy with your death."

"Not necessarily."

He countered, "I wouldn't leave it until you're on your deathbed to find out. Some people, you know, lose the power of speech then. Or it is too late for all kinds of other reasons."

"You're suggesting I won't want to return to myself?"

"It's impossible for either of us to predict how you will feel in six months' time."

I nodded.

He noticed me looking at him. "You are wondering if—"

"Of course."

"I am," he replied, glancing at Ralph. "We both are. New-bodies."

"And ordinary people going about their business out there"—I pointed somewhere into the distance—"are called Oldbodies?"

"Perhaps. Yes. Why not?"

"These are words that will eventually be part of most people's everyday vocabulary, you think?"

"Words are your living," he said. "Bodies are mine. But I would imagine so."

"The existence of Newbodies, as you call them, will create considerable confusion, won't it? How will we know who is new and who old?"

"The thinking in this area has yet to be done," he said. "Just as there has been argument over abortion, genetic engineering, cloning, and organ transplants, or any other medical advances, so there will be over this."

"Surely this is of a different order," I said. "Parents the same age as their children, or even younger, for instance. What will that mean?"

"That is for the philosophers, priests, poets, and television pundits to say. My work is only to extend life."

"As an educated man, you must have thought this over."

"How could I work out the implications alone? They can only be lived."

"But—"

We batted this subject back and forth until it became clear even to me that I was playing for time.

"I was just thinking . . ." said Ralph. He was smiling. "If I were dead we wouldn't be having this conversation."

The doctor said, "Adam's is a necessary equivocation." He turned to me. "You have to make a second important decision."

I guessed this was coming. "It won't be so difficult, I hope."

"Please, follow me."

The doctor, accompanied by a porter and a young nurse, took me and Ralph down several corridors and through several locked doors. At last we entered what seemed like a broad, low-ceilinged, neon-lit fridge with a tiled floor.

I was shivering as I stood there, and not only because of the temperature. Ralph took my arm and began to murmur in my ear, but I couldn't hear him. What I saw was unlike anything I had seen before; indeed, unlike anything anyone had ever seen. This was no longer amusing speculation or inquisitiveness. It was where the new world began.

"Where do you get them?" I asked. "The bodies."

"They're young people who have, unfortunately, passed away," said the doctor.

Stupidly, I said, as though I were looking at the result of a massacre, "All at once?"

"At different times, naturally. And in different parts of the world. They're transported in the same way as organs are now. That's not difficult to do."

"What is difficult about this process now?"

"It takes time and great expertise. But so does cleaning a great painting. The right person has to do it. There are not many of those people yet. But it can be done. It is, of course, something that was always going to happen."

Suspended in harnesses, there were rows and rows of bodies: the pale, the dark, and the in-between; the mottled, the clear-skinned, the hairy and the hairless, the bearded, and the large-breasted; the tall, the broad, and the squat. Each had a number in a plastic wallet above the head. Some looked awkward, as though they were asleep, with their heads lolling slightly to one side, their legs at different angles. Others looked as though they were about to go for a run. All the bodies, as far as I could see, were relatively young; some of them looked less like young adults than older children. The oldest were in their early forties. I was reminded of the rows of suits in the tailor's I'd visit as a boy with my father. Except these were not cloth coverings but human bodies, born alive from between a woman's legs.

"Why don't you browse?" said the surgeon, leaving me with the nurse. "Choose a short list, perhaps. Write down the numbers you fancy. We can discuss your choices. This is the part I enjoy. You know what I like to do? Guess in advance who I think the person will choose, and wait to see whether I am right. Often I am."

Shopping for bodies: it was true that I had some idea what I was looking for. I knew, for instance, that I didn't want to be a fair, blue-eyed blond. People might consider me a beautiful fool.

"Can I suggest something?" said Ralph. "You might, for a change, want to come back as a young woman."

I said, "A change is as good as a rest, as my mother used to say."

"Some men want to give birth. Or they want to have sex as a woman. You do have one of your male characters say that in his sexual fantasies he's always a woman."

"Yes . . . I see what you mean . . ."

"Or you could choose a black body. There's a few of those," he said with an ironic sniff. "Think how much you'd learn about society and . . . all that."

"Yes," I said. "But couldn't I just read a novel about it?"

"Whatever. All I want is for you to know that there are options. Take your time. The race, gender, size, and age you prefer can only be your choice. I would say that in my view people aren't able to give these things enough thought. They take it for granted that tough guys have all the fun. Still, you could give another body a run-out in six months. Or are you particularly attached to your identity?"

"It never occurred to me not to be."

He said, "One learns that identities are good for some things but not for others. Here."

"Jesus. Thanks."

I took the bag but wasn't sick. I did want to get out of that room. It was worse than a mortuary. These bodies would be reanimated. The consequences were unimaginable. Every type of human being, apart from the old, seemed available. The young must have been dying in droves; maybe they were being killed. I would make a good but expeditious choice and leave.

When the others fell back discreetly I walked beside this stationary army of the dead, this warehouse of the lost, examining their faces and naked bodies. I looked, as one might look too long at a painting until its value—the value of life—seemed to evaporate, existing only as a moment of embodied frustration between two eternities. Then I began to think of poetry and children and the early morning, until it came back to me, why I wanted to go on living and why it might, at times, seem worth it.

I considered several bodies but kept moving, hoping for something better. At last, I stopped. I had seen "my guy." Or rather, he had seemed to choose me. Stocky and as classically handsome as any sculpture in the British Museum, he was neither white nor dark but lightly toasted, with a fine, thick penis and heavy balls. I would, at last, have the body of an Italian footballer: an aggressive, attacking midfielder, say. My face resembled that of the young Alain Delon with, naturally, my own brain leading this combination out to play for six months.

"That's him," I said, across the lines of bodies. "My man. He looks fine. We like each other."

"Do you want to see his eyes?" said the nurse, who'd been waiting by the door. "You'd better."

"Why not?"

"Look, then," she said.

She pried open my man's eyelids. The room was scrupulously odorless, but as I moved closer to him I detected an antiseptic whiff. However, I liked him already. For the first time, I would have dark brown eyes.

"Lovely." I considered patting him on the head, but realized he would be cold. I said to him, "See you later, pal."

On the way out, I noticed another heavy, locked door. "Are there more in there? Is that where they keep the second-division players?"

"That's where they keep the old bodies," she said. "Your last facility will be in there."

"Facility?" I asked. The necessity for euphemism always alerted me to hidden fears.

"The body you're wearing at the moment."

"Right. But only for a bit."

"For a bit," she repeated.

"No harm will come to it in there, will it?"

"How could it?"

"You won't sell it?"

"Er . . . why should we?" She added, "No disrespect intended. If, after six months, you change your mind, or you just don't turn up, we will nullify the facility, of course."

"Right. But I would like to see where I'm going to be hanging out—or up, rather."

I moved toward the door of this room. The porter barred my way with his strong arm.

The nurse said, "Confidential."

Ralph intervened. "It's unlikely, Adam, but you might know the people. Some say they're emigrating, others 'seem' to have died. Others have disappeared, but they come here and reemerge as Newbodies."

"How much of this 'coming and going' is there about?" I asked.

Ralph didn't reply. I felt myself becoming annoyed.

I said, "It is curious, inquisitive types like me you claimed you wanted as 'initiates.' Now you won't answer my questions."

"Be a patient patient. Soon you'll have as much time on your hands as you could want. You will come to understand much more then." He embraced me. "I'll leave you now. I will visit you when it's done."

"I'll feel like a new man."

"That's right."

I was put into bed then, in my room, and examined by the doctor and his assistant. The doctor was whistling, and I closed my eyes. My body had already become just an object to be worked on. I imagined my new body being taken from its rack and prepared in another room.

After a while, the doctor said, "We're ready to go ahead now. You made a good choice. Your new facility has almost been picked out a few times now. He's been waiting a while for his outing. I'm glad his day has finally come."

Insofar as it was possible, I had got used to the idea that I might die under the anesthetic, that these might be my last moments on earth. The faces of my children as babies floated before me as I went under. This time, though, I was afraid in a new way: not only of death, but of what might come out of it—new life. How would I feel? Who would I be?

3

A THEORY-LOVING friend of mine has an idea that the notion of the self, of the separate, self-conscious individual, and of any autobiography which that self might tell or write, developed around the same time as the invention of the mirror, first made en masse in Venice in the early sixteenth century. When people could consider their own faces, expressions of emotion and bodies for a sustained period, they could wonder who they were and how they were different from and similar to others.

My children, around the age of two, became fascinated by their own images in the looking glass. Later, I can remember my son, aged six, clambering onto a chair and then onto the dining table in order to see himself in the mirror over the fireplace, kissing his fingers and saying, as he adjusted his top hat, "Masterpiece! What a lucky man you are, to have such a good-looking son!" Later, of course, they and their mirrors were inseparable. As I said to them: Make the most of it, there'll be a time when you won't be able to look at yourself without flinching.

According to my friend, if a creature can't see himself, he can't mature. He can't see where he ends and others begin. This process can be aided by hanging a mirror in an animal's cage.

Still only semi-conscious, I began to move. I found I could stand. I stood in front of the full-length mirror in my room, looking at myself—or whoever I was now—for a long time. I noticed that other mirrors had been provided. I adjusted them until I obtained an all-around view. In these mirrors I seemed to have been cloned as well as transformed. Everywhere I turned there were more me's, many, many more new me's, until I felt dizzy. I sat, lay down, jumped up and down, touched myself, wiggled my fingers and toes, shook my arms and legs, and, finally, placed my head carefully on the floor before kicking myself up and standing on it—something I hadn't done for twenty-five years. There was a lot to take in.

It was a while ago, in my early fifties, that I began to lose my physical vanity, such as it was. I've been told that as a young man I was attractive to some people; I spent more time combing my hair than I did doing equations. Certainly I took it for granted that, at least, people wouldn't be repelled by my appearance. As a child, I lived among open fields and streams, and ran and explored all day. For the past few years, however, I have been plump and bald; my heart condition has given me a continuously damp upper lip. By forty I was faced with the dilemma of whether my belt should go over or under my stomach. Before my children advised me against it, I became, for a while, one of those men whose trousers went up to their chest.

When I first became aware of my deterioration, having had

it pointed out by a disappointed lover, I dyed my hair and even signed on at a gym. Soon I was so hungry I ate even fruit. It didn't take me long to realize there are few things more risible than middle-aged narcissism. I knew the game was up when I had to wear my reading glasses in order to see the magazine I was masturbating over.

None of the women I knew could give up in this way. It was rare for my wife and her friends not to talk about botox and detox, about food and their body shape, size and relative fitness, and the sort of exercise they were or were not taking. I knew women, and not only actresses, who had squads of personal trainers, dieticians, nutritionists, yoga teachers, masseurs, and beauticians laboring over their bodies daily, as if the mind's longing and anxiety could be cured via the body. Who doesn't want to be more desired and, therefore, loved?

In contrast, I tried to dissociate myself from my body, as if it were an embarrassing friend I no longer wanted to know. My pride, my sense of myself, my identity, if you will, didn't disappear; rather, it emigrated. I noticed this with my friends. Some of them had gone to the House of Lords; they sat on committees. They were given "tribute" evenings; they picked up awards, medals, prizes, and doctorates. The end of the year, when these things were handed out, was an anxious time for the elderly and their doctors. Prestige was more important than beauty. I imagined us, as if in a cartoon, sinking into the sludge of old age, dragged down by medals, our only motion being a jealous turn of the head to see what rewards our contemporaries were receiving.

Some of this, you will be delighted to hear, happened to me. My early plays were occasionally revived, most often by

arthritic amateurs, though my latest play hadn't been produced: it was considered "old-fashioned." Someone was
working on a biography, which, for a writer, is like having a
stonemason begin to chisel one's name into a tombstone. My
biographer seemed to know, better than I did, what had been
important to me. He was young; I was his first job, a tryout.
Despite my efforts, we both knew my life hadn't been scan-
dalous enough for his book to be of much interest.

However, I'd written my memoirs and made money out of
two houses I'd bought, without much thought, in the early
1960s, one for my parents and one for myself, which turned
out to have been situated in an area that became fashionable.

Lately, what I have wanted to be cured of, if anything, was
indifference, slight depression or weariness; of the feeling that
my interest in things—culture, politics, other people, myself—
was running down. A quarter of me was alive; it was that part
which wanted a pure, unadulterated "shot" of life.

I wasn't the only one. A successful but melancholic friend,
ten years older than me, described his head as a "raw wound";
he was as furious, pained, and mad as he had been at twenty-
five. No Nirvanic serenity for him; no freedom from ambition
and envy. He said, "I wouldn't know whether you should go
gentle into that night or rage against the dying of the light. I
think, on reflection, that I'd prefer the gentle myself." But it is
as if your mind is inhabited by a houseful of squabbling rela-
tives, all of whom one could gladly eject, but cannot.

But where to find consolation? Who will teach us the wisdom we require? Who has it and could pass it on? Does it even
exist?

There was religion, once, now replaced by "spirituality,"

or, for a lot of us, politics—of the "fraternal" kind; there was culture, now there is shopping.

When I came round after the operation these weary thoughts, which I'd carried around for months, weren't with me. I had more important things to do, like standing on my head! Without Ralph telling me this—he had become an optimist—I had expected to feel, at least, as if I'd been beaten up. I had anticipated days of recovery time. However, even though I was only semi-conscious, I found I could move easily.

Nevertheless, as soon as I lay down on the bed, I fell asleep again. This time I dreamed I was at a railway station. When I take a train I like to get to the station early so as to watch the inhabited bodies move around one another. Yet I have become slightly phobic about others' bodies. I don't like them too close to me; I can't touch strangers, friends, or even myself. In the dream, when I arrived at the station everyone wanted to meet me; they crowded around me, shaking my hand, touching, kissing, and stroking me in congratulation.

This semi-sleep continued. Somehow, I became aware that I was without my body. It might be better to say I was suspended between bodies: out of mine and not yet properly in another. I was assaulted by what I thought were images but which I realized were really bodily sensations, as if my life were slowly returning, as physical feeling. I had always taken it for granted that I was a person, which was a good thing to be. But now I was being reminded that first and foremost I was a body, which wanted things.

In this strange condition, I thought of how babies are close to their mother's skin almost the whole time. A body is the child's first playground and his first experiences are sensual. It doesn't take long for children to learn that you can get things from other bodies: milk, kisses, bottles, caresses, slaps. People's hands are useful for this, as they are for exploring the numerous holes bodies have, out of which leaks different stuff, whether you like it or not: sweat, shit, semen, pus, breath, blood, saliva, words. These are holes into which you can put things, too, if you feel like it.

My mother, a librarian, was fat and couldn't walk far. Movement disturbed her. Her clothes were voluminous. She had no dealings with diets, except once, when she decided to go on a fast. She eschewed breakfast. By lunchtime she had a headache and dizziness; she was "starving" and had a cream bun to cheer herself up.

Mother was always hungry, but I guess she didn't know what she was hungry for. She replied, when I asked her why she consumed so much rubbish, "You never know where your next meal is coming from, do you?" Things can seem like that to some people, as if there is only scarcity and you should get as much down you as you can, though it never satisfies you.

Mother never let me see her body or sleep beside her; she didn't like to touch me. She didn't want anyone's hands on her, saying it was "unnecessary." Perhaps she made herself fat to discourage temptation.

As you get older, you are instructed that you can't touch just anyone, nor can they touch you. Although parents encourage their children in generosity, they don't usually share their genitals, or those of their partner, with you. Sometimes you are not even allowed to touch parts of your own body, as if they don't quite belong to you. There are feelings your body is forbidden to generate, feelings the elders don't like anyone having. We consider ourselves to be liberals; it is the others who have inexplicable customs. Yet the etiquette of touching bodies is strict everywhere.

Every body is different, but all are identical in their uncontrollability: bodies do various involuntary things, such as crying, sneezing, urinating, growing, or becoming sexually excited. You soon find that bodies can get very attracted to and repelled by other bodies, even—or particularly—when they don't want to be.

I grew up after the major European wars, playing soldier games on my father's farm. My mind was possessed by images of millions of upright male bodies in identical clothes and poses. The world these men made was mayhem and disorder, but at least, as my father used to say, they were "well turned out" for it. At school, it seemed that each teacher had a particular disability—one ear, one leg or testicle, or some war wound—which fascinated us. None of us thought we'd ever be down to just one of anything where there was supposed to be two, but we couldn't stop thinking about it. This was the misunderstanding of education: the teachers were interested in minds, and we were interested in bodies. It was the bodies I wanted when I grew up.

I became aware of the reality of my own death at the same time I became aware of the possibility of having real sex with others. Each made the other possible. You might die, but you could say "hello" before you went.

In the countryside, there are fewer bodies and more distance between them. I came to the city because the bodies are closer; there is heat and magnetism. The bodies jostle; is that for space, or for touching? The tables in the restaurants and pubs are more adjacent. On the trains and in the tubes, of course, the bodies seem to breathe one another in, which must be why people go to work. The bodies seem anonymous, but sometimes any body will do. Why would anyone want this, particularly a semi-claustrophobic like me?

If other people's bodies get too much for you, you can stop them by stabbing or crucifixion. You can shoot or burn them to make them keep still or to prevent them saying words that displease you. If your own body gets too much—and whose doesn't?—you might meditate yourself into desirelessness, enter a monastery or find an addiction that channels desire. Some bodies are such a nuisance to their owners—they can seem as unpredictable as untamed animals, or the feeling can overheat and there's no thermostat—that they not only starve or attempt to shape them, but they flagellate or punish them.

As a young man, I wanted to get inside bodies, not just with a portion of my frame, but to burrow inside them, to live in there. If this seems impractical, you can at least get acquainted with a body by sleeping next to it. Then you can put bits of your body into the holes in other bodies. This is awful fun. Before I met my wife, I spent a while putting sensitive areas of my body as close to the sensitive areas of other bodies as I could, learning all I could about what bodies wanted. I never lost my fearful fascination with women's bodies. The women seemed to understand this: that the force of our desire made us crazy and terrified. You could kill a woman for wanting her too much.

The older and sicker you get, the less your body is a fashion item, the less people want to touch you. You will have to pay. Masseurs and prostitutes will caress you, if you give them money. How many therapies these days happen to involve the "laying-on of hands"? Nurses will handle the sick. Doctors spend their lives touching bodies, which is why young people go to medical school. Dentists and gynecologists love the dark inside. Some workers, as in shoe shops, can get to hold body parts without having had to attend anatomy lectures. Priests and politicians tell people what to do with their bodies. People always choose their work according to their preferences about bodies. Careers advisers should bear this in mind. Behind every vocation there is a fetish.

Around puberty, people begin to worry—some say women do this more than men, but I'm not convinced—about the shape and size of their bodies. They think about it a lot, though the sensible know their bodies will never provide the satisfaction they desire because it is their appetite rather than their frame that bothers them. Having an appetite, of course, alters the shape of your body and how others see it. Starvation; fasting; dieting. These can seem like decent solutions to the problem of appetite or of desire.

The appetite of my new body seemed to be reviving, too. I was coming round because I was aware of a blaze of need. But my form felt like a building I'd never before been in. Where exactly was this feeling coming from? What did I want? At least I knew that my stomach must have been empty. First, I would wake up properly; then I could eat.

My watch was on the bedside table. I could see the numbers with perfect vision, but the strap wouldn't fit around my thick new wrist. At least I knew it was morning and I'd slept through the night. It was time for breakfast. I could not walk out of the room in my new body without preparation.

I continued to examine myself in the mirror, stepping forward and backward, examining my hairy arms and legs, turn-ing my head here and there, opening and closing my mouth, looking at my good teeth and wide, clean tongue, smiling and frowning, trying different expressions. I wasn't just handsome, with my features in felicitous proportion. The nurse had asked me to examine my eyes. I saw what she meant. There was a softness in me, a wistfulness; I detected a yearning, or even something tragic, in the eyes.

I was falling in love with myself. Not that beauty, or life itself, means much if you're in a room on your own. Heaven is other people.

The door opened and the surgeon came in.

"You look splendid." He walked around me. "Michelan-gelo has made David!"

"I was going to say Frankenstein has just—"

"No joins or bumps either. Do you feel well?"

"I think so."

But my voice sounded unfamiliar to me. It was lighter in tone, but had more force and volume than before.

"Go and have a pee," he said.

In the toilet, I touched my new penis and became as engrossed in it as a four-year-old. I weighed and inspected it. I raised my arms and wriggled my hips; no doubt I pouted, too. Elvis, of course, had been one of my earliest influences, along with Socrates. When I peed, the stream was full, clear, and what I must describe as "decisive." Putting my prick away, I gave it a final squeeze. Who wouldn't want to see this! My, what a lot I had to look forward to! My appetite—all my appetites, I suspected—had reached another dimension.

"Okay?" he said.

I nodded. We went into another room, where the doctor affixed various parts of me to machines, giving me, or my new body, a thorough checkup. As he did so, I babbled away in my new voice, mostly childhood memories, listening to myself in the attempt to draw myself back together again.

"I'm through," he said at last. Denying me the privacy of a natural-born being, he watched me clumsily put on the clothes Ralph had bought me. "Good. Good. This is incredible. It has worked."

"Why the surprise? Haven't you done this before?"

"Of course. But each time it seems to be a miracle. We have another success on our hands. Everything is complete now. Your mind and the body's nervous system are in perfect coordination. You have your old mind in a new body. New life has been made."

"Is that it?" I said. "Don't I require more preparation?"

"I expect you do," he said. "Mentally. There will be shocks ahead, adjustments to be made. It would be a good idea to discuss it with Ralph, your mentor. It goes without saying that you cannot talk freely about this. Otherwise you are free to go, sir. Your clock has been restarted, but it is still ticking. See you in six months. You know where we are."

"But do I know where I am?"

"I hope you will find out. I look forward to hearing how it went."

The nurse, in reception, handed me my wallet and the bag of things Ralph had told me I'd need for the first few hours after my "transformation." She took a copy of my memoirs from under the desk and asked me to sign it.

"I've long been an admirer, sir."

Writing my old name with my new fingers I had to bend over from a different height. For the first time in years, I did so without having to adjust my posture to avoid an expected pain. I stood back and stared at my signature, which resembled a bad forgery of my own scrawl. I took another piece of paper and scribbled my name again and again. However hard I tried, I couldn't make it come out like the old one.

The amused nurse called a cab for me.

I waited on the couch with my new long legs stuck out in front of me, taking up a lot of room and touching my face. Watching her work in reception, it occurred to me that the desirable nurse—whose attractiveness was, really, only lack of any flaw—might be seventy or ninety years old. Like people who work at a dentist's, and always have perfect teeth, she was bound to be a Newbody herself. But why would she be doing such a job?

A long-haired, model-like young woman approached the desk, requesting a taxi. Her hip, slightly Hispanic look was so ravishing I must have audibly sighed, because she smiled. It was difficult to tell whether she was in her late teens or early thirties. It occurred to me that we were making a society in which everyone would be the same age. I noticed that the woman was carrying an open bag in which I glimpsed what looked like the corner of a pink flannel nightgown. She sat opposite me, waiting too, nervously. In fact, she seemed to relate strangely to herself, as I must have done, moving different parts of herself experimentally, at first diffidently and then with some internal celebration. Then she smiled in my direction with such radiant confidence I thought of suggesting we share a cab. What a perfect couple we would make!

But I wanted to be back among ordinary people, those who decayed and were afraid of death. I got up and canceled the cab. I would enjoy walking. A marathon would be nothing. The nurse seemed to understand.

"Good luck," I said to the woman.

I headed for the main road. I must have walked for five miles, taking considerable strides and loving the steady motion. My new body was taller and heavier than my last "vessel," but I felt lighter and more agile than I could recall, as though I were at the wheel of a luxury car. I could see over the heads of others on the street. People had to look up to me. I'd been bullied as a kid. Now, I could punch people out. Not that a fight would be the best start to my new incarnation.

I found a cheap café and ate a meal. I ate another meal. I checked into a big, anonymous hotel where a reservation had already been made. I found a good position in the bar where I could look out for people looking at me. Was that woman smiling in my direction? People did glance at me, but with no more obvious interest than they had before. My mind felt disturbingly clear. What defined edges the world had! It had been a long time since I'd had such undeviating contact with reality. After a couple of drinks, I gained even more clarity along with a touch of ecstasy, but I didn't want to get blotto on my first day as a Newbody.

I was waiting in the crowded hotel foyer when Ralph hurried in and stood there looking about. It was disconcerting when he didn't recognize the writer he'd worshipped, whose words he'd memorized, the one he believed deserved immortality! It took him a few distracted moments to pick my body out among the others, and he still wasn't certain it was me.

I went over. "Hi, Ralph, it's me, Adam."

He embraced me, running his hands over my shoulders and back; he even patted my stomach.

"Great hard body, pal. You look superb. I'm proud of you. You've got guts. How do you feel?"

"Never better," I said. They were my words, but my voice was strong. "Thanks, Ralph, for doing this for me."

"By the way," he said. "What's your name?"

"Sorry?"

"You'll need a new name. You could keep your old name, of course, or a derivative. But it might cause confusion. You're not really Adam anymore. What do you think?"

My instinct was to change my name. It would help me remember that I was a new combination. Anyway, hybrids were hip.

"What will it be?" he asked.

"I'll be called Leo Raphael Adams," I said at last. "Does that sound grand enough?"

"Up to you," he said. "Good. I'll tell them. You have money, don't you?"

"As you insisted, enough for six months."

"I'll make sure you receive a passport and driving license in your new name."

"That must be illegal," I said.

"Does that worry you?"

"I'm afraid so. I'm not a good man by any means, but I do tend toward honesty in trivial matters."

"That's the least of it, man. You're in a place that few other humans have ever been before. You're a walking laboratory, an experiment. You're beyond good and evil now."

"Right, I see," I said. "The identity theorists are going to be busy worrying about this one."

He touched my shoulder. "You need to get laid. It works, doesn't it—your thing?"

"I can't tell you how good it feels not to piss in all directions at once or over your own new shoes. As soon as I get an erection, I'll call."

"The first time I had sex in my new body, it all came back. I was with a Russian girl. She was screaming like a pig."

"Yeah?"

"I knew, that night, it had been worth it. That all those years, day after day, watching my wife die, were over. This was moving on in glory."

"My wife isn't dead. I hope she doesn't die while I'm 'away.'"

"It's okay to be unfaithful," he said. "It isn't you doing it."

We talked for a bit, but I felt restless and kept bouncing on my toes. I said I wanted to get out and walk, shake my new arse, and show off. Ralph said he had done the same. He would let me go my own way as soon as he could. First, we had to do some shopping. Ralph had brought a suit, shirt, underwear, and shoes to the hospital, but I would need more.

"My son only seems to possess jeans, T-shirts, and sunglasses," I said. "Otherwise I have no idea what twenty-five-year-olds wear."

"I will help you," he said. "I only know twenty-five-year-olds."

I was photographed for my new passport, and then Ralph took me to a chain store. Each time I saw myself in the changing-room mirror I thought a stranger was standing in front of me. My feet were an unnecessary distance from my waist. Recently, I'd found it difficult to get my socks on, but I'd never been unfamiliar with the dimensions of my own body before. I'd always known where to find my own balls.

I dressed in black trousers, white shirt, and raincoat, nothing fashionable or ostentatious. I had no desire to express myself. Which self would I be expressing? The only thing I did buy, which I'd always wanted but never owned before, was a pair of tight leather trousers. My wife and children would have had hysterics.

Ralph left to go to a rehearsal. He was busy. He was pleased with me and with himself, but his job was done. He wanted to get on with his own new life.

Staring at myself in the mirror again, attempting to get used to my new body, I realized my hair was a little long. Whichever "me" I was, it didn't suit me. I would customize myself.

There was a hairdresser's near my house, which I had walked past most days for years, lacking the courage to go in. The people were young, the women with bare pierced bellies, and the noise horrendous. Now, as the girl chopped at my thick hair and chattered, my mind teemed with numerous excitements, wonderments, and questions. I had quickly agreed to become a Newbody in order not to vacillate. Since the operation, I had felt euphoric; this second chance, this reprieve, had made me feel well and glad to be alive. Age and illness drain you, but you're never aware of how much energy you've lost, how much mental preparation goes into death.

What I didn't know, and would soon find out, was what it was like to be young again in a new body. I enjoyed trying out my new persona on the hairdresser, making myself up. I told her I was single, had been brought up in west London, and had been a philosophy and psychology student; I had worked in restaurants and bars, and now I was deciding what to do.

"What do you have in mind?" she asked.

I told her I was intending to go away; I'd had enough of London and wanted to travel. I would be in the city for only a few more days, before setting off. As I spoke, I felt a surge or great push within, but toward what I had no idea, except that I knew they were pleasures.

Walking out of the hairdresser's, I saw my wife across the road pulling her shopping cart on wheels. She looked more tired and frailer than my mental picture of her. Or perhaps I was reverting to the view of the young, that the old are like a race all of whom look the same. Possibly I needed to be reminded that age in itself was not an illness.

I recalled talking in bed with her last week, semi-asleep, with one eye open. I could see only part of her throat and neck and shoulder, and I had stared at her flesh thinking I had never seen anything more beautiful or important.

She glanced across the street. I froze. Of course her eyes moved over me without recognition. She walked on.

Being, in a sense, invisible, and therefore omniscient, I could spy on those I loved, or even use and mock them. It was an unpleasant loneliness to which I had condemned myself. Still, six months was a small proportion of a life. What would be the purpose of my new youth? I had led a perplexed and unnecessarily pained inner life, but unlike Ralph, I had not felt unfulfilled, or wished to be a violinist or pioneering explorer or to learn the tango. I'd had projects galore.

My bewilderment was, I guessed, the experience of young people who'd recently left home and school. When I taught young people "creative" writing, their excessive concern about "structure" puzzled me. It was only when I saw that they were referring to their lives as well as to their work that I began to understand them. Looking for "structure" was like asking the question: What do you want to do? Who would you like to be? They could only take the time to find out. Such an experiment wasn't something I'd allowed myself to experience at twenty-five. At that age I moved between hyperactivity and enervating depression—one the remedy, I hoped, for the other.

If my desire pointed in a particular direction this time around, I would have to discover what it was—if there was, in fact, something to find. Perhaps in my last life I'd been over-constrained by ambition. Hadn't my needs been too narrow, too concentrated? Maybe it was not, this time, a question of finding one big thing but of liking lots of little ones. I would do it differently, but why believe I'd do it better?

That evening I changed hotels, wanting somewhere smaller and less busy. I ate three times and went to bed early, still a little groggy from the operation.

The next day was a fine one, and I awoke in an excellent mood. If I lacked Ralph's sense of purpose, I didn't lack enthusiasm. Whatever I was going to do, I was up for it.

There I was, walking in the street, shopping for the trip I had finally decided to take, when two gay men in their thirties started waving and shouting from across the road.

"Mark, Mark!" they called, straight at me. "It's you! How are you! We've missed you!"

I was looking around. There was no one else they could have been motioning to. Perhaps my leather trousers were already having an effect on the general public. But it was more than that: the couple were moving through the traffic, their arms extended. I considered running away—I thought I might pretend to be jogging—but they were almost on me. I could only face them as they greeted me warmly. In fact, they both embraced me.

Luckily, their talk was relentless and almost entirely about themselves. When I managed to inform them that I was about to go on holiday, they told me they were going away too, with friends, an artist and a couple of dancers.

"Your accent's changed, too," they said. "Very British."

"It's London, dear. I'm a new man now," I explained. "A reinvention."

"We're so pleased."

I understood that the last time we met, in New York, my mental state hadn't been good, which was why they were pleased to see me out shopping in London. They and their circle of friends had been worried about me.

I survived this, and soon we were saying our farewells. The two men kissed and hugged me.

"And you're looking good," they added. "You're not modeling anymore, are you?"

"Not at the moment," I said.

One of them said, "But you're not doing the other thing, are you, for money?"

"Oh, not right now."

"It was driving you crazy."

"Yes, yes," I said. "I believe it was."

"Shame the boy band idea didn't work out. Particularly after you got through the audition with that weird song."

"Too unstable, I guess."

"Would you like to join us for a drink—of orange juice, of course? Why not?"

"Yes, yes," said the other. "Let's go and talk somewhere."

"I'm sorry, but I must go," I said, moving away. "I'm already late for my psychiatrist! He tells me there's much to be done!"

"Enjoy!"

I rang Ralph straight away.

"You got your erection, eh?" he said.

I insisted on seeing him. He was rehearsing. He made me go to the college canteen during his tea break and wait. When he did turn up, he seemed preoccupied, having had an argument with Ophelia. I didn't care. I told him what had happened to me on the street.

"That shouldn't have occurred," he said, with some concern. "It's never happened to me, though I guess I'll start to get recognized when I've played Hamlet."

"What is going on? Don't they do any checks first?"

"Of course," he said. "But the world's a small place now. Your guy's from L.A."

"Mark. That's his name. That's what they called me."

"So? How can anyone be expected to know he's got friends in Kensington?"

"Suppose he's wanted by the police somewhere?"

He shook his head. "It won't happen again," he said confidently. "The chances of such a repeat are low, statistically."

"There have been other weird occurrences."

"For example?" He didn't want to hear, but he had to.

"Tell me, first, how did he die, my body, my man?"

Ralph hesitated. "Why do you want to know?"

"Why, are you not allowed to tell me?"

"This is a new area."

I went on, "In bed, I was aware of these twinges, or sensations. There were times in my Oldbody life, particularly as I got older, or when I was meditating, when I felt that the limits of my mind and body had been extended. I felt, almost mystically, part of others, an 'outgrowth of the One.'"

"Really?"

"This is different. It's as if I have a ghost or shadow soul inside me. I can feel things, perhaps memories, of the man who was here first. Perhaps the physical body has a soul. There's a phrase of Freud's that might apply here: the bodily ego, he calls it, I think."

"Isn't it a little late for this? I'm an actor, not a mystic."

I noticed a lack of respect in Ralph. I was a puling twenty-five-year-old rather than a distinguished author. It hadn't taken long before I was confronted with the losses involved in gaining prolonged youth.

I said, "I need to know more about my body. It was Mark's face they were seeing when they looked at me. It was his childhood experience they were partly taking in, not yours or mine."

"You want to know why he snuffed himself out? I'm telling you, Leo, face it, this is the truth and you know it already. Your guy's going to have died in some grisly fashion."

"What sort of thing are we talking about?"

"If he's young, it's not going to be pleasant. No young

death is a relief. The whole world works by exploitation. We all know the clothes we wear, the food, it's packed by Third World peasants."

"Ralph, I am not just wearing this guy's shoes."

"He was definitely 'obscure,' your man. There's no way I'm going to let them give you shoddy goods. Anyway, it's impossible, at the moment, to just go and kill someone for their body. Their family, the police, the press, everyone's going to be looking for them. The body has to be 'cleared,' and then it has to be prepared for new use by a doctor who knows what he is doing. It's a long and complicated process. You can't just plug your brain into any skull, thank Christ. Imagine what a freak show we'd have then."

"If he's been 'cleared,' I think that at least you should tell me what you know," I said. "I presume he was homosexual."

"Why else would he be in such good shape? Most hets, apart from actors, have the bodies of corpses. You object to homosexuality?"

"Not in principle, and not yet. I haven't had time to take it in. I'm at the beginning here. I need to know what all this might mean."

Ralph said, "As far as I know, he was nutty but not druggy. A suicide, I think, by carbon monoxide poisoning. They had to fix up his lungs. I looked into it for you, Adam—Leo, I mean. I asked them to give you the best. Some of those women were in great shape."

"I told you, I'm not ready to be a woman. I'm not even used to being a man."

"That was your choice, then. Your man had something like clinical depression. Obviously a lot of young people suffer from it. They can't get the help they need. Even in the long run they don't come round. Antidepressants, therapy, all that, it never works. They're never going to be doers and getters like us, man. Better to be rid of them altogether and let the healthy ones live."

"Live in the bodies of the discarded, you mean? The neglected, the failures?"

"Right."

"I see what you're getting at. 'Mark' might have suffered in his mind. He might not have lived a 'successful' life, but his friends seemed to like him. His mother would like to see him."

"What are you saying?"

"What if I—"

"Don't think about pulling that kind of stunt in front of his mother," he said. "She'd go mad if you walked in there with that face on. His whole family! They'd think they'd seen a fucking ghost!"

"I'm not about to do that," I said. "I don't know where she lives. That's not quite what I mean."

Ralph said, "My guy was struck by lightning while lying drunk under a tree. Nothing unusual about my man, thank Christ, though I keep away from AA meetings."

There wouldn't be much more I could get out of Ralph. I had to live with the consequences of what I'd done. Except that I had no idea what those consequences might turn out to be.

Ralph said, "You will come and see me as Hamlet?"

"Only if you come and see me as Don Giovanni."

"Yeah? Is that what you're going to do? I can see you as the Don. Got laid yet?"

"No." He gave me my new passport and driving license.

"Listen, Ralph," I said as we parted. "I need you to know I'm grateful for this opportunity. Nothing quite so odd has ever happened to me before."

"Good," he said. "Now go and have a walk and calm down."

I was, I noticed, becoming used to my body; I was even relaxing in it now. My long strides, the feel of my hands and face, seemed natural. I was beginning to stop expecting a different, slower response from my limbs.

There was something else.

For the first time in years, my body felt sensual and full of intense yearning; I was inhabited by a warm, inner fire, which nonetheless reached out to others—to anyone, almost. I had forgotten how inexorable and indiscriminate desire can be. Whether it was the previous inhabitant of this flesh, or youth itself, it was a pleasure that overtook and choked me.

From the start of our marriage I had decided to be faithful to Margot, without, of course, having enough idea of the difficulty. It is probably false that knowing is countererotic and the mundane designed to kill desire. Desire can find the smallest gap, and it is a hell to live in close proximity to and enforced celibacy with someone you want and with whom contact, when it occurs, is of an intimacy to which one has always been addicted. I learned that sexual happiness of the sort I'd envisaged, a constant and deep satisfaction—the romantic fantasy we're hypnotized by—was as impossible as the idea that you could secure everything you wanted from one person. But the alternative—lovers, mistresses, whores, lying—seemed too destructive, too unpredictable. The overcoming of bitterness and resentment, as well as sexual envy of the young, took as much maturity as I could muster, as did the realization that

you have to find happiness in spite of life. I became a serial
substituter: property, children, work, raking the garden leaves
kept the rage of failure at bay. Illness, too, was helpful. I
became so phobic of others I couldn't even have a stranger cut
my hair. My daughter would do it. This is how I survived my
life and mind without murdering anyone. Enough! It was not
enough.

Now I found myself looking at young women and even
young men on the street and in cafés. When, on my way down
an escalator, a woman on her way up smiled and gestured at
me, I pursued her into the street. I would, this time, follow my
impulses. I approached her with a courage I'd never had as a
young man. Then, my desire had been so forceful and
strange—which I experienced as a kind of chaos—I'd found it
difficult to contain or enjoy. For me to want someone had
meant to get involved in maddening and intense negotiations
with myself.

I asked the girl to join me for a drink. Later, we walked in
the park before retiring to her room in a cheap hotel. Later
still, we ate, saw a film, and returned to her room. She loved
my body and couldn't get enough of it. Her pleasure increased
mine. She and I looked at and admired each other's bodies—
bodies that did as much as two willing bodies could do, several
times, before parting forever, a perfect paradigm of impersonal
love, both generous and selfish. We could imagine around each
other, playing with our bodies, living in our minds. We became
machines for making pornography of ourselves. I hoped
there'd be many more occasions like it. How fidelity interferes
with love, at times! What were refinement and the intellect
compared to a sublime fuck?

As we lay in each other's arms, and, when she was asleep, I kissed her and said, "Goodbye, whoever you are," creeping out at dawn to walk the streets for a couple of hours, it occurred to me that this was an excellent way to live.

4

NEXT MORNING I was on the train to Paris, my new rucksack on the rack above me. Before we reached Dover I had helped people with their heavy luggage, eaten two breakfasts, and read the newspapers in two languages. For the rest of the journey I studied guidebooks and timetables.

For a few weeks before I became a Newbody, I had been in what I called an "experimental" frame of mind. After finishing *Too Late*, I'd been failing as a writer. I'd become more skillful, but not better. I wouldn't have minded the work getting worse if I'd been able to find interesting ways to make it more difficult. Urgency and contemporaneity make up for any amount of clumsiness, in literature as in love. I had stopped work and had been drawing, taking photographs, and talking to people I'd normally flee. I would see what occurred, rather than hide in my room. Despite these efforts, there was no doubt I was becoming isolated, as if it were the solitude of my craft I had become attached to, and it was that I couldn't get away from.

There are few things more depressing than constant pain, and there were certain physical agonies I thought I would never be without. Flannery O'Connor wrote, "Illness is a place where there is no company." Perhaps I had been unconsciously preparing for death, as I recall preparing for my parents' deaths. I realized what a significant part of my life my own death had become. As a badly off young man I had constantly thought: Do I have the money to do this? As an older man I had constantly thought: Do I have the time for this; or, Is this what I really want to do with my remaining days?

Now, a renewed physical animation, combined with mental curiosity, made me feel particularly energetic. In this incarnation I would go everywhere and see everything.

When I first had children I was inspired to think about my own childhood and parents; now this transformation was making me reflect on the sort of young man I had been. I hadn't traveled much then. I had been too absorbed in the theater, working in any capacity, reading scripts, running the box office, and serving tyrannical directors. The rest of the time I was having tragic, complicated affairs and trying to write. I forfeited a lot of pleasure for my craft; at times I found the deferment and discipline intolerable. I'd break out and go mad, before retiring to my room for long periods—for too long, I'd say now. But those years of habit and repetition served me well: I gained invaluable experience of writing, not only of the practical difficulties but of the terrors and inhibitions that seem to be involved in any attempt to become an artist.

My excitements then had never been pure; they had always

been anxieties. In later life I wondered whether I had been too constrained and afraid for my future, too focused on the success I yearned for and too determined to become established. Traveling unworriedly through Europe had been the least of my concerns.

Did I regret it now, or wish it otherwise? At least I had the sense to understand that there couldn't be a life without foolishness, hesitation, breakdown, unbearable conflict. We are our mistakes, our symptoms, our breakdowns.

The thing I missed most in my new life was the opportunity to discuss—and, therefore, think about properly—the implications of becoming a Newbody. I doubted whether Ralph would have been interested in going into it further. Perhaps such a transformation, like face-lifts, worked better for people who didn't have theories of authenticity or the "natural," people who didn't worry about its meaning at the expense of its obvious pleasures.

It was its pleasures I was in search of. Soon, I was tearing across Paris; then I went to Amsterdam, Berlin, Vienna. I did the churches and museums of Italy, and they did me. It wasn't long before I'd had my fill of degraded, orgasmically violated bodies strung from walls, and vaults full of old bones. On most days I woke up in a different place. I traveled by train and bus, in the slowest possible way. Sometimes I just walked across mountains, beaches, or fields, or got off trains when I fancied the view from the window. If I liked a bus—the route, the thoughts it provoked, the width of the seat, or a sentence in a book I was reading on it—I'd sit there until the end of the line. There was no rush.

I stayed in cheap hotels, hostels, and boarding houses. I had money, but I didn't want opulence. As a young man I'd wanted that—as a measure of success and of how far I had escaped my childhood. Now it seemed confining to be over-concerned with furnishings.

I talked only to strangers, making friends easily for the first time in years. I met people in cafés, museums, and clubs, and went to their houses when I could. If I had been too fastidious before, now I stayed with anyone who would have me, to see how they lived. Unlike most young people, I was interested in people of all ages. I'd go to the house of a Dutch guy of my age, and end up chatting to his parents all weekend. It was the mothers I got along with because I was interested in children and how you might get through to them. The mothers talked about children, but I learned they were talking about them-selves, too, and this moved me.

I did, at least, know how to look after myself. I could escape anyone boring. People were more generous than I had noticed. If you could listen, they liked to talk. Perhaps being ambitious and relatively well known from a young age had put the barrier of my reputation, such as it was, between me and others.

The days in each city were full. I could drink, have sex with people I picked up or with any prostitute whose body took my fancy, visit galleries, queue for cheap seats to the theater or opera, or merely read and walk. In the former East Berlin all I did was walk and take photographs. In a bar in Paris, I met a young Algerian guy who modeled occasionally. The male models didn't earn anything like as much as the girls, and most of them had other jobs. My friend got me a catwalk show dur-ing Fashion Week, and I took my turn parading on the narrow

aisle, as the flashbulbs exploded and the unprepossessing jour-
nalists scribbled. Was it the clothes or really the bodies they
were looking at? Backstage, it was a chaos of semi-naked girls
and boys, dressers, the designer, and numerous assistants.

I enjoyed all of it, and after chatting with the designer,
whom I'd known slightly in my previous body, I was offered a
job in one of his shops, with the prospect of becoming a buyer,
which I declined. I did ask him, though, whether, by any
chance, as I was a "student," he'd read any of "my"—Adam's—
books or seen "my" plays or films. If he had, he couldn't
remember. He didn't have time for cultural frivolity. Making a
decent pair of trousers was more important. He did say he liked
"me"—Adam—though he had found me shy at times. He said,
to my surprise, that he envied the fact that women were
attracted to me.

The following day, my new catwalk acquaintance thought
it would be a good idea to take me shopping. I had told him I
had a small inheritance to blow, and he knew where to shop. In
our new gear we went to bars suitable for looking at others as
we enjoyed them looking at us—those, that is, who didn't
regard us dark-skinners with fear and contempt.

I didn't stay; I wasn't like these kids. I didn't want a place
in the world and money. One day, because it rained, I thought
I should go to Rome. There, as I attended a lecture and dozed
in the front row in my new linen suit, the queer biographer of
an important writer, leaning over me enormously, asked me
out for a drink. At dinner, this British hack said he wanted me
to be his assistant, which I did agree to try, while insisting, as
I'd learned I had to, that I would not be his lover. He claimed
that all he wanted was to lick my ears. I thought: Why not

share these fine pert ears around? They're not even mine, but a general asset. I closed my eyes and let his old tongue enjoy me. It was as pleasant as having a snail crawl across your eyeball. It was more difficult being a tart than I'd hoped. Tarts are trouble, mostly to themselves.

I could experiment because I was safe. If you know you're going home, you can go anywhere first. I went with him, imagining tall, glass-fronted bookcases and long, polished library tables on which I would work on my version of *The Key to All Mythologies,* in the way I'd browsed in my father's books as a teenager. That, indeed, was what I was doing, "browsing" or "grazing" in the world. The job was less demanding than I'd hoped. Mostly it involved me wearing the clothes he bought for me to parties and dinners. I was his bauble or pornography, to be shown off to friends—intelligent, cultured queens I'd have liked to talk with. As a young man I didn't much enjoy the company of my peers; I liked being an admired boy in the theater, surrounded by older men.

Therefore this fantasy of Greek life suited me, except that my "employer" refused to let me out of his sight. When I did get the opportunity to read in his library, I could see his bald pate bobbing up and down outside, as he tried to watch me through the window from an uneven box. His adoration of me became nothing but suffering for him, until I began to feel like an imprisoned princess from *The Arabian Nights.* Beauty sets people dreaming of love. If you don't want to be in someone else's dream you have to clear off.

I got a job working as a "picker" at the door of a club in Vienna. I tended to point at the inpulchritudinous and lame until a lunatic kicked me in the stomach. A few days later, having been taken to a casino by another acquaintance, I was boredly smoking a cigarette outside and wondering why people were so keen to rid themselves of their money when a woman came to me. She said she'd been watching me. She liked my eyes. She wanted to make love to me.

She was not old. I must have been looking doubtful. (I wasn't always sure whether my expression matched my feeling. I wasn't, yet, convinced of my ability to lie.)

"I will pay you," she said.

"Have you paid for such love before?"

She shook her head. My deal with myself was not to turn down such offers. I looked at her more closely and said no one had ever offered me a better exchange.

"Come, then."

She had a chauffeur, and she took me with her. I sat in the back of the car, being driven through the night to an unknown destination.

She was an American heiress with a partially collapsed villa outside Perugia. She hired an octogenarian pianist to play Mozart sonatas out of tune while she painted me nude looking out at the olive groves. Few portraits can have taken longer. I listened to her for days and strode about in shorts and workmen's boots, pretending I could mend things, though everything seemed fine as it was. (Is it only in Italy that ruin itself can seem like art?)

There were always her eyes to return to. I still liked having people fall in love with me. There are moments of life you get addicted to, that you want over and over, but then you get frustrated when you can't go any further, when the thing you've most wanted bores you.

My real labor was at night, in her room, where, after taking hours to prepare for me, she'd await my knock. I went at my employment seriously, limbering up, bathing, meditating, a proud professor of satisfaction. What internal trips I took, pretending to be a dancer or rock climber. It was dangerous work, sex, but, as always, it was the terrors and uncertainties that made it erotic. For her there had to be safety at the end, some hours of peace in her mind. I looked out for this on her face when she was asleep, like a blessing, and was pleased, waiting beside the bed to assess her temperature, her hand in mine. Then I would sleep well, alone. My pleasure was in her pleasure. After a few weeks, she wanted me to live with her in New York, if Italy got too slow for me. It did, but I didn't. I could satisfy her, but only at the cost of disappointing her. I walked away in my boots through the olive trees. Her eyes were on my back; she did not know where her next love would come from, if at all.

I was glad to have the time to walk around the cities, listening to music, always my greatest passion, on my headphones, particularly as, in my previous body, I'd been suffering from some deafness. I went to clubs and made the acquaintance of DJs. I talked about music. But to be honest, in my former guise I could get to meet more interesting people.

However, I loved this multiplicity of lives; I was delighted with the compliments about my manner and appearance, loved being told I was handsome, beautiful, good-looking. I could see what Ralph meant by a new start with old equipment. I had intelligence, money, some maturity, and physical energy. Wasn't this human perfection? Why hadn't anyone thought of putting them together before?

Like many straights, I'd been intrigued by some of my gay friends' promiscuity, the hundreds or even thousands of partners. A gay actor I knew had once said to me, "Anywhere I go in the world, one glance and I can see the need. A citizen of nowhere, I inhabit the Land of Fuck." I'd long admired and coveted what I saw as the gay's innovative and experimental lives, their capacity for pleasure. They were reinventing love, keeping it close to instinct. Meanwhile, at least for the time being—though it was changing—the straights were stuck with the old model. I had, of course, envied all that sex without a hurting human face, and in my new guise I had plenty of open bodies in close proximity. On one particular day and night I had sex with six—or was it seven?—different people. It's not something you'd want to do often. Once in a lifetime might just do it.

In Switzerland, through a woman I'd been talking to in a bar, I became acquainted with a bunch of kids in their late twenties who were making a film about feckless young people like themselves. I helped the group move their equipment and was interested to see how they used the new lightweight cameras their parents had financed.

They began to shoot long scenes of banal, everyday dialogue. I was never one to believe that Andy Warhol's films could be a fruitful model, but I encouraged them to keep the camera still and photograph only the faces of their subjects, letting them speak while I sat behind the camera, asking questions about their childhood. I took these away to a studio, cut some of them together, and put music on. The best version was one where I took the sound of the voices off altogether, but kept the music going. The unreachable, silent, moving mouths—someone trying to be heard, or not being attended to—were oddly affecting. When it was my turn in front of the camera I had myself painted white, with a black stripe down the middle, and called it "zebra piece." One night, we showed the films in a club and the naked zebra danced on stage with a local thrash band.

Others in the group, operating from a collapsing warehouse, were curating shows of contemporary art. Some reasonable things did get done, though no one much noticed. It was irritating when I found myself interested in them as a teacher or parent—the extent of their minds; in how seriously they could take themselves. They didn't read much; there was a lot of cultural knowledge I took for granted and they didn't. My own son didn't start to read or watch decent films until he was almost twenty. He wouldn't allow us, but only a female teacher, to turn him on to these pleasures. Recently, on the radio I'd said I considered reading about as important as raising poodles. As intended, this had got me into wonderful trouble with the bookworms. The whispering, worshipful tones in which my parents referred to "literature" and "scholarship" had always made me wonder what more could be done with a body than pass information into and out of it.

I had been to a club once, in the early 1990s, to see Prince, with my son and the college lecturer who seemed to be educating him (in bed), Deedee Osgood. Despite the squalor and the fact that everyone but me was virtually naked and on drugs, I loved looking at everyone. Now, most evenings, my new pals took me to clubs. This soon bored me, so they gave me Ecstasy for the first time. Though I had smoked pot and taken LSD, and known people who'd become junkies or cocaine addicts, alcohol was the drug of my generation. It seemed the best drug. I'd never understood why anyone would want to waltz with mephitic alligators.

I doubted whether any of my new acquaintances went a day without a smoke or some other stimulant. As my friends knew, the E hit me as a revelation and I wanted it served to the prime minister and pumped into the water supply. I popped handfuls of it every day for a fortnight. It led me into my own body and out into others', insofar as there was anyone real there at all. I couldn't tell. (I liked to call us E-trippers "a loose association of solipsists.") My ardor made my new pals laugh. They had learned that E wasn't the cure, and the last thing the world needed was another drug philosopher.

But after the purifications and substitutions of culture, I believed I was returning to something neglected: fundamental physical pleasure, the ecstasy of the body, of my skin, of movement, and of accelerated, spontaneous affection for others in the same state. I had been of puny build, not someone aware of his strength, and had always found it easier to speak of the most intimate things than to dance. As a Newbody, however, I began to like the pornographic circus of rough sex; the stuff that resembled some of the modern dance I had seen, animalistic, without talk. I begged to be turned into meat, held down, tied, blindfolded, slapped, pulled, and strangled, entirely merged in the physical, all my swirling selves sucked into orgasm. "Insights from the edge of consciousness," I'd have called it, had words come easily to me at that time. But they were the last thing on my mind.

By using others, I could get myself on a sexual high for two or three days. It was indeed druglike: a lucent, shivering pleasure not only in my own body but, I believed, in all existence at its most elemental. Narcissus singing into his own arse! Hello! I was also aware, as I danced naked on the balcony of a house overlooking Lake Como at daybreak after spending the night with a young couple who didn't interest me, of how many addicts I'd known and how tedious any form of addiction could be. The one thing I didn't want was to get stuck within.

For the group, there was sex of every variety, and the others' drug-taking had moved to heroin. At least two of the boys were HIV positive. Several of the others believed that that was their destiny. Because my contact with reality was, at the most, glancing, it took me a while to see how desperate the pleasures were, and how ridiculously romantic their sense of shared tragedy and doom was. My generation had been through it, with James Dean, Brian Jones, Jim Morrison, and others. If I'd been a kid now, I'd have found poetic misery hard to resist. As it was, I knew I was not of them, because I couldn't help wondering what their parents would have thought.

What we used to call "promiscuity" had always bothered me. Impersonal love seemed a devaluation of social intercourse. I couldn't help believing, no doubt pompously, that one of civilization's achievements was to give value to life, to conversation with others. Or was faithful love only an unnecessarily constraining bourgeois idiocy?

There would be a moment when the other, or "bit of the other," as we used to say, would turn human. Some gesture, word or cry would indicate a bruised history or ailing mind. The bubble of fantasy was pricked. (I came to understand fantasy as a fatal form of preconception and preoccupation.) I saw another kind of opening then, which was also an opportunity for another kind of entry—into the real. I fled, not wanting my desire to take me too far into another person. Really, apart from with the woman who paid me, when it came to sex I was interested only in my own feeling.

It has, at least, become clear that it is our pleasures, rather than our addictions and vices, that are our greatest problems. Pleasure can change you in an instant; it can take you any-where. If these gratifications were intoxicating and almost mystical in their intensity, I learned, when something stranger happened, that indulgence wasn't a full-time job and reality was a shore where dreams broke. It turned out I was seducible.

One of the artists in my group had a four-year-old son. The others were only intermittently interested in him, as I was in them, and mostly the kid watched videos. His loneliness reflected mine. If I'd been up partying and couldn't sleep the next day, I would, before I cured my comedown with another pill, take him to see the spiders in the zoo. Making him laugh was my greatest pleasure. We played football and drew and sang. I didn't mind ambling about at his speed, and I made up stories in cafés. "Read another," he'd say. He helped me recall moments with my own children: my boy, at four, fetching me an old newspaper from the kitchen, as he was used to my per-petual reading.

With his stubborn refusals, the kid reduced me twice to fury. I found myself actually stamping my feet. This jarring engagement made me see that otherwise I was like a spy, con-cealed and wary. If my generation had been fascinated by what it was like to be Burgess, or Philby or Blunt—the emotional price of a double life, of hiding in your mind—the kid reminded me of how much of one's useful self one locked away in the keeping of serious secrets.

The kid sent me into an unshareable spin. I wept alone, feeling guilty at how impatient I had been with my own children. I composed a lengthy email apologizing for omissions years ago, but didn't send it. Otherwise, I saw that most of my kids' childhood was a blank. I had either been somewhere else or wanted to be, doing something "important" or "intellectually demanding." Or I wanted the children to be more like adults— less passionate and infuriating, in other words. The division of labor between men and women had been more demarcated in my day: the men had the money and the women the children, a deprivation for both.

I came to like the kid more than the adults. One time, finding me puking on the floor, he was kind and tried to kiss me better. I didn't want him to consider me a fool. The whole thing shook me. I hadn't expected this Newbody experience to involve falling in love with a four-year-old whose narcissism far exceeded my own. When it came to youth and beauty, he had it all, as well as his emotional volume turned right up. It hadn't occurred to me that if I wanted to begin again as a human being, it would be as a father, or that I would have more energy with which to miss my children living at home, their voices as I entered the house, their concerns and possessions scattered everywhere. Ralph had failed to warn me of feeling "broody." I guessed such an idea would recommend "eternal life" to no more than a few, just as you never hear anyone say that in heaven you have to do the washing-up while suffering from indigestion. I had to shut the possibility of fatherhood out of my mind, kiss the kid goodbye, and remind myself of what I had to look forward to, of what I liked and still wanted in my old life.

In my straighter moments, despite everything, I wanted to be close to my wife. I liked to watch her walk about the house, to hear her undress, to touch her things. She would lie in bed reading and I would smell her, moving up and down her body like an old dog, nose twitching. I still hadn't been all the way around her. Her flesh creased, folded, and sagged, its color altering, but I had never desired her because she was perfect, but because she was she.

After my journey through the cities and having to leave the kid, I decided to roam around the Greek islands. My own vanity bored even me and I craved warm sun, clear water, and a fresh wind. I'd had two and a half months of ease and pleasure, and I wanted to prepare for my return—for illness and death, in fact. I began to think of what I'd tell my friends I'd been doing.

As the doctor had predicted, I wasn't looking forward to reentering my old body. When I ate, would it still feel as though I were chewing nails and shitting screws? On some days, would I still be able to swallow only bananas and painkillers? But as my old body and its suffering stood for the life I had made, the sum total of my achievement made flesh, I believed I should reinhabit it. I was no fan of the more rigid pieties, but it did seem to be my duty. Would most deaths soon feel like suicides? It was almost funny: becoming a Newbody made living a quagmire of decision. In the meantime, I was looking forward to staying in the same place for a few weeks and finishing, or at least beginning again, *Under the Volcano*.

My father, the headmaster of a local school, said, before he died of heart failure, that he'd always regretted not becoming a postman. A gentle job, he believed, wandering the streets with nothing but dogs to worry about, would have extended his life. Idiotic, I considered this: worrying was an excitement I needed. But now I had some idea what he meant.

Not that he'd have survived on a postman's salary. I had begun to realize that I, too, wasn't used to today's financial world. I'd always bought my own milk, but had no idea of the price. I'd seriously underestimated what I'd need as a Newbody. The price of condoms! Apart from the cash I'd put aside for my return trip, I'd spent most of my money and couldn't use my bank accounts or credit cards. Until my return I needed a cheap place to stay and money for my keep.

It was in Greece, on a boat one morning, that I met a middle-aged woman with a rucksack who was going to study photography at a "spiritual center" on the island I was visiting. She had hitchhiked from London to visit the Center, which was known to be particularly rejuvenative for those suffering from urban breakdown. When I told her my sad story, she offered to take me along with her.

While I waited in a café in a nearby square, drinking wine and reading Cavafy, she went to the Center and inquired whether there was any work I could do in exchange for food, a place to sleep, and a little payment. Otherwise, I would find a job in a bar or disco and crash on the beach. The woman returned and told me the Center had been looking for an "oddjob" to clean the rooms and work in the kitchen. Providing the leader didn't dislike me, I would eat for free, earn a little money, and sleep on the roof.

We walked down to a handful of flower-dotted, white-washed buildings on the edge of an incline, with a view of the sea. She opened the door in a long, high wall.

"Look," she said. I did: the devil peeping into paradise. "They must be between classes."

It was a shaded garden where the women—naturally, it was mostly women—sat on benches. They talked, wrote earnestly in notebooks, and read. In one corner, a woman was singing; another was doing yoga, another combing her hair; on a massage table, a body was being kneaded.

Here, these middle-aged, middle-class, and, of course, divorced women from London took "spiritual" nourishment, meditation, aromatherapy, massage, yoga, dream therapy. What baby with its mother ever had it better than in this modern equivalent of the old-style spa or sanatorium? The three men I saw were middle-aged, with hollow chests and varicose veins.

She asked, "Will you be all right here?"

"I think I'll manage," I replied.

After being shown around the kitchen, the "work" rooms, and the dining room, I was taken to see the Center's founder or leader, the "wise woman," as she was called, without irony, or with none that I noticed. I had the impression that it would be wise for me, too, to lay off the irony. It was too much of a mature and academic pleasure.

Patricia came to the door of a small, shuttered house ten minutes' walk from the Center. In her late fifties, she was big, with long, graying hair, in clothes with the texture and odor of cheap oriental carpets. She invited me in and ordered me to sit on a cushion. As I dozed off, she talked loudly on the phone, read her correspondence ("Bastards! Bastards!"), scratched her backside, and, from time to time, looked me over.

When I got up to inspect a picture, she turned. "Sit down, don't fidget!" she said. "Be still for five minutes!"

I sat down and bit my lip.

I could recall her variety of feminism from the first time around: its mad ugliness, the forced ecstasy of sisterhood, the whole revolutionary puritanism. I didn't loathe it—it seemed to me to be a strain of eccentric English socialism, like Shavianism—as long as I didn't have to live under or near it. It did, however, seem better being a young man these days: the women were less aggressive, earned their own money, and didn't blame anyone with a cock for their nightmares.

I was irritated by what I considered to be this woman's high-handed approach, and was about to walk out—not that she would have minded—when it occurred to me that for her I was virtually a child as well as only a potential menial. I was neither an Oldbody nor a Newbody. I was a nobody.

I'd always had a penchant for tyrants, at school, at work, and in the theater where, when I was young, they flourished, having come from army backgrounds. I had enjoyed testing myself against them. How many times could they beat you up before they had to come to terms with you? However, now I was shaken by a blast of late-adolescent fury. I'd forgotten how adults talk down to you, when they're not ignoring you, and how they hate to hear your opinion while giving their own. You're at one of your parents' dinner parties and your parents' friends ask you how your exams are going and you tell them you have failed and you are glad, glad, glad. Your parents tell you not to be rude, and you've just been to see

If . . . Your parents want a gin and tonic but you want a machine gun and the revolution, and you want them now.

Despite this, I guessed that Patricia had an intelligence and intensity my former persona would have enjoyed. I liked the fact that the one thing I wouldn't have said about her, even after only cursory inspection, was that she was serene. Long periods of inner investigation and deep breathing, or whatever therapy she practiced, hadn't seemed to have cured her of irritability or incipient fury.

When she did look at me, with what I was afraid was some perception, I felt I would shrivel up. For the first time I felt that someone had seen me as an impostor, a fake, as not being what I seemed. The game was up, the pretense was over.

"What did you say your name was?" she asked.

"Leo Raphael Adams."

She snorted. "Arty, bohemian parents, eh?"

"I suppose so."

"I probably knew them."

"You didn't."

"What did they do?"

"Lots of things."

"Lots of things, eh?"

"They moved around a lot."

"Good for them," she said. "What do you want to do?"

"Work here for a bit," I replied. "I'll do anything you want me to."

"I should hope so. But don't pretend to take what I say literally, Leo, when you know I mean 'in life.'"

"In life? I don't know," I said genuinely. "I've no idea. Why do I have to 'do' anything?"

She imitated me. "Don't know. Don't care. Don't give a shit."

I shaded my eyes, as if from the sun. "Why do you keep staring at me?"

"Your blank face."

I said, "Is it blank? I've looked at it a lot and—"

"I can imagine, dear."

"I've never thought of it as blank."

"Is there one intelligent thought in there—something that will make me think, 'I haven't heard that before'? I must have forgotten," she went on, "that conversation isn't a male art."

There was a lot I did want to say, but if I started on at her I wouldn't know what it was like to be young.

I said, "You want me to leave."

"Only if you want to." She started to giggle. "We don't usually have men working here, though there's no rule against it. I may be an old-style sixties feminist, and the self-esteem of women in a male world may be of interest, but it wasn't my intention to set up a nunnery. Your porky prick"—she looked directly at my crotch—"will certainly put the cat among the pigeons. I think that will amuse me. You can stay . . . for a bit."

"Thank you."

Patricia went to the window, leaned out, and yelled into the square.

"Alicia!" she called. "Alicia!" Almost immediately, a girl appeared. "Take him away," she said. "He's working here at the moment. Give him something to do!"

As I walked back, I was aware of someone beside me, as insubstantial and insistent as a shadow.

"I think I'll get out of here," I said.

"Is that what you normally do—run?"

"If I'm feeling sensible."

"Don't start getting sensible."

I said, "Something about me seemed to enrage her."

"You take it personally?"

"I've decided to."

"Why?"

"It made me wonder what sort of power I might have over her."

"You'll never have any power over her."

Alicia was not a girl, but a young woman from London, a frail poet with a squint and a roll-up in the corner of her mouth. She told me she had been staying at the Center for three months, at the expense of an American benefactor, writing and teaching. Despite the relentless sunlight and the hunger for it of the other women, Alicia had not tanned. Her skin remained remorselessly "Camden High Street in the rain," as I thought of it. She was to show me the roof of the Center, where I would sleep. It was baking during the day and most likely cold at night, but it suited me, being secluded. I like the sky, though until now have lacked the time to "commune" with it.

While I unpacked my few things, Alicia opened a spiral notebook, coughed her soul out, tore at her nails with her teeth, and asked whether I minded hearing her poetry.

"Why not?" I said. "I haven't had any contact with poetry since I was at school."

"Where were you at school?"

"All over the place."

"Read anything?"

"Toilet walls."

She warned me: her poetry was mostly about things.

"Things?"

She explained that even here, "in the cradle of consecutive thought," the language of the New Age and of self-help, now beyond parody, had taken over the vocabulary of emotional feeling and exchange. If the language of the self was poisoned, it was disastrous for a poet. This was yet to happen to objects without souls, on which she had decided to concentrate her powers.

"Give me an example," I said.

She began with a poem about kettles and toasters. I liked it, so she followed up with another about her Hoover, and with a further one about stereo systems, which was unfinished. When I asked her to go on, she told me what the others were to be about—carpets, beds, curtains—and requested suggestions for more.

I changed my shirt, a moment I always enjoyed, and said I thought one about windows would be good.

"Windows?" she said. "What are you talking about?"

"What's wrong with windows?"

She explained that it was "too poetic" a subject. Quoting John Cage, she said she was interested in the "white" emotions rather than the "black" ones. She needed to get past the "black" ones to the "white" ones.

"D'you see?"

"Not a word of it. Me, I'm only the cleaner."

"That's who I'm writing for. Cleaners and crooks—I mean cooks. Some poems open only for the ignorant."

"I must be your man, then."

She was looking at me. Her face was pale but unmarked, as

though her despair had neglected to invade it. Yet now one of her eyes was twitching like a trapped butterfly. I wanted to go to her and press my finger against it. But maybe I would have just pulled it off and torn it to pieces. The poor girl must have fallen in love at that moment.

The work I had to do at the Center was hard. My body was uncomplaining—it liked being stretched and exerted—but my mind kicked up a fuss. In a life devoted to myself, it had been years since I'd been forced to do anything against my will. I'd always been reasonably successful at getting women to look after me. Now I helped with the cooking; it was good to learn to cook. I emptied the bins and carried heavy sacks of food from the vans; I was taught how to build a wall. I swept, cleaned, and painted the rooms. I guessed that this was what the world was like for most people, and it didn't harm me to be reminded of it.

I came to appreciate the simplest things. I grew a beard and learned t'ai chi, yoga, and how to play a drum. I swam long distances, sunbathed, read, and listened to the women at meal-times and at night, just hanging around them, as I had my mother as a child. I cultivated a reputation for shyness and silence. I might have been a beauty, but direct attention was the last thing I craved. Sometimes I would massage the women, singing to myself. One time, I saw one of the group lying under a tree reading my last play, which was produced five years ago. As I walked past her, I said, "Any good?"

"The play's not as good as the film."

I had begun to love the beauty of the island and the peace it gave me. I was almost free of the desire to understand. Agitation and passion seemed less necessary as proofs of life. I wondered whether, when I returned to my old body, my values would be different. I had been certain that I wanted to go back, but it was a question that wouldn't leave me alone now. There were decent arguments on both sides. What could have been worse? I would put it off for as long as possible.

Patricia usually appeared at breakfast and made a speech about the purpose and aims of the Center. Once, she told us one of her dreams; then she interpreted it, to prevent any misunderstanding. There was an impressed silence before she swept away. She uttered few words in my direction but she always looked hard at me as if we were connected in some way, as if she were about to speak. I supposed she looked at everyone like this, now and again, to make them feel part of her community. I no longer believed she understood me, but did I make her particularly curious? She seemed to say: What do you really want? It agitated me. I kept away from her but she remained in my mind, like a question.

Patricia's workshops were the most popular and intense, and always full. However, as Alicia told me in confidence, they were known more for the quantity of tears shed than for the quality of wisdom transmitted. But I was only a kitchen skivvy and took no part. Taking my father's advice, I was on a working holiday.

Ten days after I'd started, Patricia came into the kitchen, where I labored under the regime of an old Greek woman with whom I could barely communicate. I'd never seen Patricia in the kitchen before. Like the obdurate adolescent I wanted her to see me as, I refused to meet her look. She had to tell me to stop peeling potatoes.

"Just stop now."

"Patricia, I wouldn't feel good about leaving half a potato."

"To hell with potatoes! I am about to begin my dream workshop with the new group. I've decided that it's time you joined us."

"Me? Why?"

"I think you should learn something."

"Oh, I don't want to learn. I had years of it and nothing went in, as you pointed out." She looked hurt, so I said, "What kind of thing is it?"

She sighed. "We free associate around people's dreams. We might write around them, or paint or draw. Or even dance. I've seen you shake your butt, at the disco. The girls were certainly intrigued, as they are when you parade around the place with your shirt off. But you keep away from the workshop members, don't you?"

"It goes without saying."

"Even that idiot with the ghost?"

"Ah, yes," I said. "That damned ghost."

The ghost always cheered Patricia up.

One of the women who'd recently come to the Center and been allocated a room in town, as some people were, had stood up at breakfast and told us her room was haunted. Typically, Patricia imagined this was a ruse for the woman to be moved to a superior room with a sea view—not something Patricia could offer or fall for. Instead of moving her, Patricia had deputed me to sit, all night, in the doorway of the woman's room, keeping an eye out for the revenant.

"Watching for ghosts is one of your duties," Patricia had said to me, barely containing her delight. "When the bastard turns up, you deal with it."

"Such work wasn't in my original job description," I said. "And do ghosts use doors?"

"Get lost and do it. Ghosts use all orifices."

I had told Alicia, "Wait 'til they hear this back in London— that I've been employed on a ghost watch."

That night, I'd stayed awake as long as I could but had, of course, fallen asleep in the chair. The ghosts came. Nothing with a sheet over its head bothered me, but my own internal shades and shadows, by far the most hideous, had become mightily busy. The woman I guarded slept well. By morning, I was in a cold sweat with rings the color of coal under my eyes. The women at the Center, when they weren't being solicitous, found they hadn't laughed as much since they'd arrived.

"Particularly not with the ghost woman," I said now to Patricia.

"Good. You're not included in the price of the holiday." She went on, "Now, come along. People pay hundreds of pounds to participate. I want you to see what goes on here. Tell me. Surely you don't believe that only the rational is real, or that the real is always rational, do you?"

"I haven't thought much about it."

"Liar!"

"Why say that?"

"There's more to you than you let on! How many kids your age whistle tunes from *Figaro* while they're peeling potatoes?"

She strode out, expecting me to follow her, but I'm not the sort to follow anyone, particularly if they want me to.

I looked at the old Greek woman, washing the kitchen floor. This was the kind of reality I was adjusted to: getting a patch of earth the way you want it while thinking of nothing.

However, I left the kitchen and, outside, went up the steps. In the large, bright room, I could see that Patricia, along with the rest of the class, had been waiting for me.

She pointed at the floor. "Sit down, then we'll start."

Around the group she went, soliciting dreams. What a proliferation of imagination, symbolism, and wordplay there was in such an ordinary group of people! I stayed for over an hour, at which point there was a break. Breathing freely at last, I hurried out into the heat. I kept going and didn't return, but went into town, where I had provisions to buy for the Center.

When I returned, Alicia was waiting under a tree outside, with her notebook. She stood up and waved in my face.

"Leo, where have you been?"

"Shopping."

"You've caused a terrible fuss. You can't walk out on Patricia like that," she said. "I kind of admire it. I like it when people are driven to leave my lessons. I know there's something pretty powerful going on. I don't like poetry to be helpful. But we masochists are drawn to Patricia. We do what she says. We never, ever leave her sessions."

"I had work to do," I said. I wasn't prepared to say that I had left Patricia's workshop because it had upset me. Dreams had always fascinated me; in London, I wrote mine down, and Margot and I often discussed dreams over breakfast.

My dream on the "ghost watch" had been this: I was to see my dead parents again, for a final conversation. When I met them—and they had their heads joined together at one ear, making one interrogative head—they failed to recognize me. I tried to explain how I had come to look different, but they were outraged by my claims to be myself. They turned away and walked into eternity before I could convince them—as if I ever could—of who I really was.

The other dream was more of an image: of a man in a white coat with a human brain in his hands, crossing a room between two bodies, each with its skull split open, on little hinges. As he carried the already rotting brain, it dripped. Bits of memory, desire, hope, and love, encased in skinlike piping, fell onto the sawdust floor, where hungry dogs and cats lapped them up.

Much as I would have liked to, I couldn't even begin to talk about this with the group. My "transformation" had isolated me. As Ralph could have pointed out, it was the price I had to pay.

I couldn't either, of course, say this to Alicia, who had become my only real friend at the Center. She came from a bohemian family. Her father had died in her early teens. At fifteen, her mother took her to live in a sex-crazed commune. It had made her "frigid." She felt as neglected as a starving child. Now she overlooked herself, eating little but carrying around a bag of carrots, apples, or bananas which she'd chop into little pieces with a penknife and devour piece by piece. She only ever ate her own food, and, I noticed, would only eat alone or in front of me.

In the evenings, she and I had begun to talk. Twice a week there were parties for the Center participants. The drinking and dancing were furious. The women had the determined energy of the not quite defeated. They liked Tamla Motown and Donna Summer; I liked the ballet of their legs kicking in their long skirts. After, it was my job to clear away the glasses, sweep the floor, empty the ashtrays, and get the Center ready for breakfast. I did it well; cleanliness had become like a poem to me. A cigarette butt was a slap in the face. Alicia liked to help me, on her knees, late at night, as the others sat up, confessing.

Alicia had begun to write stories and the beginning of a novel, which she showed me. I thought about what she was doing and commented on it when I thought I could be helpful. I liked being useful; I could see how her confidence failed at times.

In the late evenings, when I'd finished work, sometimes we went to the beach. We'd walk past couples who'd left the bars and discos to copulate in the darkness: French, German, Scandinavian, Dutch bodies, attempting, it seemed, to strangle the life out of one another. Our business seemed more important, to talk about literature. Sex was everywhere; good words were less ubiquitous.

Since my mid-twenties, I'd taught both literature and writing at various universities and usually had a writing workshop in London. I'd been interested by how people got to speak, and to speak up, for themselves, and by the effect this had on all their relationships. When it came to Alicia, some sort of instruction was something I fell into naturally, and liked.

Nevertheless, I tried to speak in young tones, as if I knew only a little; and I tried not to be pompous, as I must have been in my old body. It was quite an effort. I was used to people listening to or even writing down what I said. The pomposity was useful, for emphasis, and my authority could seem liberating to some people. Alicia seemed to like the authority I was able to muster, at times. Being older could be useful.

I had to be wary, too, of this thin, anxious girl. If she was the reason I didn't leave, when she asked me about myself and my education I was evasive, as if I didn't quite believe my own stories, or, in the end, couldn't be bothered with them, which frustrated her. She wanted more of me. I could see she knew I was holding a lot back.

"What have you been writing?" I asked now, as we walked.

"A poem about windows."

"Everyone knows poems and windows don't go together."

"They'll have to get along," she said. "Like us." Then she said, "Hurry, you've got to go and see Patricia."

"Now? Is she angry with me?"

She squeezed my hand. "I think so."

Her fear increased mine. I was reminded of all kinds of past transgressions and terrors: of my mother's furies, of being sent to the headmistress to be smacked on the hand with a ruler. In my youth, all sorts of people were allowed to hit you, and were even praised for doing it; they didn't thank you if you returned the compliment. Now, as numerous other fears arose, I went into such a spin it took me several moments to remember I was called Leo Adams. I could choose to behave differently, to revise the past, as it were, and not be the scared boy I was then.

"Come on," I said. "Walk with me."

"Aren't you afraid of her?" Alicia asked.

"Terrified."

"I am, too. Are you going to leave?"

"Well, I don't see why I shouldn't."

"Please don't." She went on, "But there is something else, too. She heard your joke."

"She did? She didn't mention it to me."

"She might now, perhaps."

"How did it get around?"

She blushed. "These things just do."

A few days ago I had made a joke, which is not a good idea in institutions. It was not a great joke, but it was on the spot and had made Alicia suddenly laugh in recognition. I had called the Center a "weepeasy." I used the word several times, as we young people tend to, and that was that. It had entered the bloodstream of the institution.

Now we walked through the village to Patricia's. The shops were closed; the place was deserted. Most people were having their siestas, as was Patricia at this time, usually.

Outside Patricia's, Alicia said she'd wait for me under a tree across the square.

I knocked on the door, and Patricia's irritable face appeared at the window. I'm glad to say I always annoyed Patricia; by being alive at all, I failed her. On this occasion, to my dismay, she brightened.

She had come to the door wearing only a wraparound skirt. Her large brown breasts were hanging down.

"My," I said, and then blushed. I knew she'd heard it as "mine." I went on, "Patricia, there's something I need to talk to you about."

"I'm glad you've come, Oddjob," she said. "I've got some work for you. Why did you leave my workshop?"

"I wanted to think about it."

"Did you enjoy it, then?" When I nodded, she said, "If so, how much? Very, very much? Just very much? Quite a lot? Or something else?"

"Let me think about that, Patricia." She was looking at me. I said, "I did like it, in fact."

"If you did really, you can say why—in your own words."

I said, "You used the dream not as a puzzle to be solved, with all the anxiety of that, as if one of us would get it right, but as a felt image, to generate thoughts or other images. That was useful. I haven't stopped thinking."

"That's a good thing to say." She was flattered and pleased. "You see, you can be almost articulate, if you really want to be. By the way, I heard what you called the Center. Weepeasy," she said. "Right?"

"Sorry," I said, bowing my head.

"Is that what you think?"

"It's easy to make people cry." I went on, "Confession, not irony, is the modern mode. A halting speech at Alcoholics Anonymous is the paradigm. But what concealments and deceptions are there in this exhibition of self-pity? Isn't it tedious for you?"

"There's no rigor here anymore, you could be right. Or any progress. It's become the same every day. I can tell you, that's the least of it." Then she said, "Please, come here."

"Sorry?"

"Here!" I shuffled forward. She put her arms around me and pressed her breasts into my body. "I am feeling tense today. I wanted to run a center for self-exploration, only to discover I'd started a small business. You can't explore anything if you don't get the figures right—the eighties taught some women that, at least. Now I'm sick of being an accountant and I'm sick of being wise. Sometimes, I only want to be mad."

"Yeah," I said. "Being the wise woman must be a right bore."

"Who takes care of me? I have to mother everyone! You've been attending the massage class, haven't you? You know how to do it."

By now she was pulling at my fingers.

"Patricia—"

"Massage me, Leo, you dear boy. There's the oil."

"I want to talk about Alicia."

"Who wants to hear about that funny little thing? Oh, talk, talk about what you want, as long as you smooth out my soul."

Her skirt dropped to the floor. She walked across the room, located the oil, and lay down on a towel on her low bed.

She was watching me scratch my stomach. There were certain conversations I'd missed in this new life. You might have a new body but if your mind is burdened the differences don't count for much.

"Go on," she said.

I told her how Alicia had got sweet on me and that I was concerned about it. I emphasized that I hadn't deliberately led her on.

Of course, I loved the attention of the women at the Center—who didn't, admittedly, have much else to look at— and had walked around barefoot, wearing only shorts. Celibacy had increased my desire; I wanted to live less in my mind. I remember Margot telling me, years ago, this thing about certain school phobics. Some boys, of particularly disturbed sexuality, imagined that their bodies had turned into penises. The dreaded school was their mother's forbidden body. I was all sex, a walking prick, a penis with an appended body. I didn't flirt; I was unprovocative. I didn't need to do anything.

In my mad mind, I became a kind of performer. Many of my friends have been actors, singers, or dancers, men and women who used their bodies in the service of art, or as art itself; people who were looked at for a living. Those of us who cannot perform, who imagine from the audience only an examination of our faults, can have little idea of the relationship between player and voyeur, of how the audience, like a sea of feeling, might hold you up, if you can use it. What do you see and hear out there in all that blackness? What are the watchers doing to you? What was the stripper or any celebrity doing but increasing and controlling envy and desire? This was a splendidly erotic activity, it seemed to me.

It had been years since I had danced, and now, since I didn't need much sleep, I danced every night in one or other of the town's discos, with women from the Center. Most of them were older than forty, some were over fifty. They knew the chances of their being loved, caressed, wanted were diminishing, even as their passion increased, in the sun. I danced with them, but I didn't touch them. If I'd been a "real" kid, I probably would have gone to bed, or to the beach, with several of them. I was their pornography, a cunt teaser. But at least everyone knew where they stood with me.

Usually, while I danced, Alicia watched me, or sat on a chair drinking and smoking. She never danced herself, but took a lot of pleasure in others' enjoyment. Oddly enough, the music most people preferred originated in my day: 1950s rock 'n' roll and 1960s soul. I knew every note. It sounded fresher and more lasting than the labored literary work of me and my contemporaries.

In one of the town's discos, while dancing with my "coven,"

as I called them, several of the local men started to taunt me. They didn't like this spoiled kid dancing with and hugging these happy women night after night, as well as looking after their bags, fetching them drinks, and making sure they all got safely back to the Center. One night, they gathered around me at the bar and said they wanted to see what sort of man I was. They could find this out only on the beach, where we would be able to have "a good talk." Alicia and the other women had to escort me out of there in a group. Looking back, I could see the men standing at the door, smoking and sneering.

Why did this happen? How did they see me? I inquired of Alicia. As someone who had everything, and a future, too. There was nothing I couldn't do or be, she seemed to think. They hated it and wanted it. They could have killed and eaten me.

There were other fantasies about me. A woman in her fifties had told Alicia that I made the women feel inadequate. I was a problem-free rich kid bumming around the world before going to work for a bank. "We're trying to restart our troubled lives here. He's just passing through," she said.

"Maybe that is what you are," Alicia continued, after she'd told me, throwing down her roll-up and rubbing out the stub with her sandal. "You have the confidence, poise, and sense of entitlement of a rich kid. Isn't that right?"

I didn't answer; I didn't know what to say. I hadn't anticipated this much envy. I had, though, known actors who'd become movie stars and been made paranoid and withdrawn as much because of the pressure of imagined spite as that of fame.

I labored over Patricia's crumpled and folded flesh, humming and thinking. I was good at this; at least I'd learned to love giving comfort and pleasure.

I said, "How can I deal with this? I am beginning to feel like an object. It is not pleasant, it's persecution."

"You are supremely enviable," she said, her voice muffled by the towel. "You're like the woman everyone wants but no one understands. What you require is support and protection."

"Who from?"

"That is up to you. But you must ask for it." She went on, "It doesn't sound as if you've done the wrong thing, Oddjob. You've made her and some of the others lovesick but you haven't misled anyone. You're a good lad. Women of Alicia's age—they'd fall in love with a plank of wood."

I was working hard at Patricia's body. To my dismay, as I punched and pummeled, she didn't seem to relax, but began breathing harder.

She turned, put out her hands, and untied the string that held up my trousers.

"Please, Patricia," I said. "Don't—"

She was holding my penis. "That's a mighty fine thing you've got there. Know how to use it?"

"No, I guess you could show me."

"You haven't slept with Alicia?"

"That's right."

"You're a good boy, then. Now, be an even better boy for me."

Her eyes were glazed with desire.

I said, "I thought you were supposed to be a wise woman?"

"Even the wise need a prick now and again. You've been fluttering your eyelashes at me for days, don't think I haven't noticed. I'm very intuitive. Now, can you follow through?"

I didn't want to disappoint her; I didn't want her to feel her age or resent me.

Her hands were rough, and at one point I wondered whether she might be wearing gloves. I remembered that for exercise she liked to build stone walls. But, to my surprise, I became excited.

Her noises were honest and forthright. I was sitting facing her. We were rocking. I must have been holding my breath. "Breathe, breathe," she ordered. I did what she said. She went on. "Relax and breathe from your stomach, that way you'll hold out longer."

It worked, of course. When I'd relaxed, she said, "Now, continue."

Patricia howled, "Adore me, adore me, you little shit!"; she dug her fingers into me, scratched and kicked me, and, when she came, thrust her tongue into my mouth until I almost gagged.

"I needed that," she said at last. She was lying on the bed, legs apart, almost steaming. "Dear boy, do fetch me a glass of water."

I took it to her.

"Thanks, Oddjob. A job well done, eh?"

I sat on the end of the bed and said, "Now you'll be able to give an orgasm workshop."

"You know," she said, "a lot of the women here think you're a haughty little kid. I don't mind that. I like it. I could humble you, you know."

"Thank you, Patricia," I said. "I think you just have. I'd better go now."

"One more thing," she said.

Patricia opened her legs and, from the end of the bed, had me look at her masturbate busily. At times her entire hand seemed to disappear into her body, as if she were about to turn herself inside out.

"Bet you haven't seen that before," she murmured.

"No," I said sourly. "One lives and learns."

She was about to fall asleep. She waved me away, but not before saying, "You come back here tonight. Bring your things. Everything will be better if you come and live here."

"Why would that be?"

"This is the best room in the village. See you tonight!"

I scurried away across the square. Alicia called after me, caught me up, and put her arm through mine.

"You're still here?"

"But why not?"

"Alicia, I'm on my way to the beach."

"Are you okay? Can't I come with you?"

I didn't like to make her run behind me, but I needed to wash myself. I knew she was still there because she was shouting out poems—not her own—as we went, to remind me of the good things.

I stripped off and ran into the sea. I swam and jogged on the beach until I was exhausted. I lay down next to her with the sun on me. Soon, I'd dozed off. When I opened my eyes, she was sitting there wearing just a cigarette, her arms hugging her knees. Unlike the other women at the Center, she never removed her clothes but always wore a long-sleeved top and ankle-length skirt.

"What is it?"

She said, "You slept with her." Her hands shook as she

drew on her cigarette. "Everyone in this hemisphere will have heard."

"But you didn't cover your ears."

"I listened to your music. Every note."

"What will you do with what you heard? Write about it—or is it too human for you?"

"If that was all I was capable of, I'd hate myself!" She took my hand and placed it on her foot. "Will you look at me? We can't have sex. You don't want to. Perhaps you've had more than enough for today. I have never had an orgasm, and I am a virgin. Touch me, if you feel like it." She lay back. "Would you?"

After my earlier experience, I couldn't claim to be erotically absorbed. I did begin to rub her with the palms of my hands; then, when I began to stroke her with my fingers and her eyes closed, my mind began to wander.

"I need to borrow this."

I took her notebook and pen, and began to make an inventory of what I found on her flesh. I did this, as they say on television, in no particular order. I went to what interested me.

The first thing I noticed was a light brown eyelash on her throat, one of her own. On her forehead there was one hard spot and one pus-filled, with several others under the skin. Her hair looked as though it had been dyed a while ago; parts of it had been bleached by the sun. It was hard to make out its original color. Her lips were a little ribbed and sore, the bottom more than the top.

I found a purplish bruise, recent, on her side where, perhaps, she had knocked into a table. On her knees there were three little childhood scars. I ran my fingers along the still-livid scar where, I guessed, she'd had her gallbladder removed. She had five painted toenails, all chipped, and five, on the other foot, unpainted: I guess she must have got bored. There was a lot of sand, mostly dry, between her toes, on the soles of her feet and instep.

She wore cheap silver earrings, but I didn't feel she was interested in personal adornment. One earlobe was slightly inflamed. I also found a leaf on her leg, several insects, dead and alive, in different places, and dirt on her leg. The skin around her fingernails had been pulled and torn. Her cheap watch told the wrong time. Her teeth seemed good, perhaps she had worn a brace as a child; but they were stained now, from smoking, and one was chipped. There were random and quite deep scratchmarks on one arm (left), which I had noticed before but hadn't attended to. They appeared to have been done with an insufficiently sharp object—a penknife, say, rather than a razor blade—as if she'd decided to doodle on herself on the spur of the moment, without preparing.

I peered into her ears and mouth, between her legs and then her toes, where I discovered another insect; I looked up her nose—surprisingly hairless, compared to mine. On her chest she had scored what I guessed to be the word *poet*. On her thigh, there were other words that had been recently bleeding.

I wrote, in the fatuous modern manner, "This Is a Person in the Here and Now Lying Down," and jotted it down, forensically, working in silence for an hour. I kept the dead insects, the leaf, a couple of pubic hairs, an example of the dirt, a smear of blood and vaginal mucus, and a record of the words inside her notebook. Mostly her eyes were closed, her breaths deep and long.

I awoke her from her "dream" and showed her what I'd been doing.

"No one's ever done a nicer thing for me," she said.

"Pleasure."

"You said to me once, 'What people want is to be known.' Can I ask you: What is that scar you have?"

"What scar? Where?"

She looked at me as though I were stupid, before pointing it out to me. It was under my elbow, in the soft flesh.

"You don't know what it is?"

"I probably do," I said, irritably. "I don't even remember where I got it."

"You don't want to know yourself. You don't know yourself as well as you know me. I don't understand that. If you knew yourself you wouldn't have done what you did with that woman."

"I don't see why we have to know either ourselves or each other."

"But what else is there?"

"Enjoying each other."

"Knowing is enjoying, for me."

These were the sort of wrangles we liked. After, we walked back in silence.

I noticed, out at sea, a large yacht with little boats carrying provisions out to it. I'd forgotten that everyone from the Center had been invited to a party on it that evening. I hadn't taken much notice at the time, but there were numerous rumors about the owner. He was either a gangster, film producer, or computer magnate. I wasn't sure which was considered to be worse. I was surprised when Patricia announced at breakfast that we were all going. I was intending to miss it; I couldn't see that Patricia would even notice my absence. How things had changed since then! Hadn't she said to me, a couple of hours ago, "See you tonight!"

I couldn't defy Patricia and remain at the Center. If I was going to leave, I'd have to know where I was going.

I said goodbye to Alicia and went to the roof to think. I discovered myself to be even more furious than before about what Patricia had done to me, and furious with myself for having failed to escape untouched. I would insist on sleeping alone tonight and leave for Athens by the first boat. I packed my bags in readiness. I was young; I could run.

5

I WENT TO eat in a taverna in town, reading at the table. After a few pages, I thought, "I can do this." I pulled some paper from my rucksack and started on a story, which offered itself to me. It was something seen, or apprehended as a whole—almost visual—which I felt forced to find words for. My hands were shaking; without literature I couldn't think, and felt stifled by a swirl of thoughts which took me nowhere new. But writing and the intricacies of its solitude was a habit I needed to break in order to stray from myself. Some artists, in their later life, become so much themselves, they go their own way, that they are no longer open to influence, to being changed or even touched by anyone else, and their work takes on the nature of obsession. Margot once said to me, "When you think or feel something important, instead of saying it, you write it down. I'd love it to rain on your computer!"

It did. I put away my pen and paper, paid, and left.

At the Center the voices, usually so quietly fervent, were almost raucous. Everyone, apart from Patricia, who had yet to appear, had gathered in colorful skirts, dresses, and wraps. Some wore bells on their ankles; many wore bras. The night air, invariably sweet, vibrated with clashing female perfumes; jewelry flashed and jingled. Excitement about the party on the yacht was so high that some people were already dancing.

I was wearing my usual shorts and white T-shirt. I'd bought this body because I liked it as it was, a pure fashion item that didn't require elaboration.

I laughed when I saw that Alicia had attempted to comb her hair, making it look even more frizzy. With the light behind her, she looked as though she had a halo. She also wore lipstick, which I'd never seen on her. It was as if she were trying out being "a woman."

"I was afraid you wouldn't come," she said.

"Me, too," I replied.

"We're on the trip, then."

"Looks like it."

Our singularity made us both seem insubordinate, as if we were refusing to enter into the spirit of the evening, which was how, to my regret, I'd been as a young man—rebellion as affectation. Not that anyone seemed to notice. With the arrival of Princess Patricia in a long tie-dyed skirt and with flowers in her hair, the party became impossible to resist.

At Patricia's entrance, I said to Alicia, "I didn't realize we were attending a film première!"

After posing in the door until everyone became silent and took her in, she came to me, kissed me on the lips, patted my face, licked her lips, and refused to acknowledge Alicia.

"Are we ready?"

She held my arm and pulled me along, telling the others to follow. It was clear: she wanted to go on the cruise because she wanted to show me off.

Patricia and I led what became a kind of procession through the village to the beach. The old men, sitting at café tables watching us pass, seemed not only to be from another era but appeared to be another kind of species altogether.

On the beach, where other foreigners from the island were gathering, a band greeted us. In the distance, the yacht, the only bright thing in the dark ocean, glittered beneath the emerging stars. Despite Patricia's attention, I was glad to be there.

Small boats carried us to the yacht. Patricia sat beside me, holding my hand. "I've been walking on air ever since our lovemaking. You were just what I needed." She kept leaning across me.

"Patricia . . ." I was going to tell her, coyly, that I didn't want things to "move along" too quickly. "I think we—"

She interrupted me. "You didn't even get changed," she said. "Hold still, then. Let me put this in." She was fiddling with my ear. "Now we have matching earrings." She patted my face, sat back, and looked at me.

I touched my ear. "Oh, yes," I said, perplexed. "I must have forgotten I'd had it pierced."

"There are several holes. What a funny boy you are," she said. "I've watched you dancing. You do it wonderfully. You must have trained somewhere."

"I did."

"Where?" She went on, "Will you dance with me all night?"

"Not all night, Patricia."

She took my hand and slipped it between her thighs. "Most of it, then, darling boy."

We were helped from the boat onto the yacht. The owner, Matte, an excitable young man, greeted us on deck.

"Thank you, Patricia, for bringing your crew! You are all welcome!" he said. He waved at the women following us. "Come along, girls! Let's get down!"

As we looked around the boat, Strauss's *Also sprach Zarathustra* in the von Karajan version began playing. I adore Richard Strauss, but am ready to admit how much great music has been turned into kitsch. Where is there to turn for something that sounds fresh today, except to the new or weird? You couldn't turn Bartók's quartets or Webern's meditations into easy listening.

Oddly, though, the Strauss didn't seem only sententious. Against the sea and sky, in this place, and taken by surprise—which, it seems to me, is often the best way to hear music; walking into a shop one Saturday morning and hearing Callas; tricked into amazement—it thrilled and uplifted me again.

This was what I, as a young man, would have wanted.

Food, drink, and sexual possibility appeared to be limitless. Matte's uniformed staff walked about with trays, some of which held sex toys and condoms. There was a disco and a band. Those people already there appeared to be British, American, and European playboys, models, actors, singers, pleasure seekers, indolent aristocrats. There were also people that even I recognized from the British newspapers, pop stars and their partners, and actors from soap operas. These were people with groovy sunglasses and ideal bodies—I guessed that different parts of their bodies were of different ages and materials—who made it clear they had seen all this before, and liked being looked at.

Alicia nudged me. "Someone's staring at you."

A young woman was indeed looking at me. I smiled, and received a timid wave.

"As always, you're popular," said Alicia. "Can I ask who it is?"

"I don't know. She looks like a movie star."

"You know movie stars?"

"Of course not, but they all know me." I returned the woman's wave. "Come on."

We all strolled around. Patricia seemed to be doing a fine impression of Princess Margaret in her heyday. Alicia and I, at least, weren't sure whether to resist or swoon at the sight of so much gold. Alicia said she liked the way English Londoners were sneery and hated to be credulous, whereas I now found that tedious. This time around I wanted to like things.

When, for a moment, Alicia went to fetch a drink, the "film star" who'd waved earlier covered herself up and hurried over.

"How funny to meet you here," she said, kissing me.

I kissed her back; I had to. But I was afraid she'd known me as "Mark"; perhaps we'd been "married." I vowed that when I next saw Ralph I would put an end to his immortality.

"Don't you know me?"

I looked at her until a picture came into my mind. It was of an old woman in a wheelchair wearing a pink flannel night-gown. This woman and I had become Newbodies on the same day. We were, in a sense, the same age.

I said, "Good to see you. How are you enjoying it?"

"I don't know. Wherever I go, people try to touch or have me. If I don't comply, they're nasty. Still," she said, "I wouldn't have men fighting over me if I were a pile of ash."

"Oh, I don't know. What else will you do?"

"I've got a record contract," she said. "And you?"

"It's strange, like being a ghost."

She glanced around. "I know. Relax now. There are others here like us. Everyone else is so silly and blind."

"How many others like us?"

I looked at the faces and bodies behind her. How would I know who was who?

"More than you think. We play tennis and we stay up late at cards, talking about our lives. We have plenty of time, you see. Like pop stars and royalty, we stick together."

I thought of them, the beauties around a table together, like moving statues, an artwork.

I said, "Soon, everyone in the world will know."

"Oh, yes, I think so. Does it matter? Come and talk to me later." She was looking down at her feet. "Do you love your body now?"

"Why shouldn't I?"

"I'm a little too tall and my waist is too thick. My feet are big. Overall, I'm not comfortable."

She left when Alicia rejoined me. "You say you don't know that woman. Will you go with her now?"

"Go where? I don't know what you're talking about."

"You can if you want," Alicia said. "There is time. We've set sail."

"Set sail for where?"

Alicia was laughing at me. "I don't know. But I do know that setting sail is what boats tend to do. We're on here until dawn."

I ran to the side of the boat. We were already in motion. It hadn't occurred to me that I wouldn't be able to escape at any time. I considered jumping into the sea, but wasn't convinced I could swim so far. Anyway, Patricia was beside me straight away. She seemed to be insisting that I stay beside her all night. Not only at her side, in fact, but within touching distance.

She was rubbing my shoulders. "I've never seen anything like you. I've never wanted anyone so much. I'd never have given myself permission to touch someone like you before." Her fist was somewhere in my head. "Where did you get that hair?"

I almost said, "I saw it in a fridge and bought it, along with everything else you like about me." I wondered whether that would matter. Now, at least, I knew something. The world is different for the beautiful. They're desired, oh yes; other bodies are all over them. But they don't necessarily like them.

"Come and see this," Patricia said, without a glance at Alicia. "A young man will be interested."

I followed her through the boat to a cabin door. She pushed it. The room within was almost completely dark.

I stepped in. It took a couple of minutes for my eyes to adjust. There must have been about thirty naked people in the room, with a greater proportion of men than women. In a corner, there were Goyaesque mounds of bodies, lost in one another. It was difficult to tell which limb belonged to which body. I wondered whether some of the limbs had become independent of selves, turning into creatures in their own right, arms dancing with legs, perhaps, and torsos alone. There was music, talking, and—a lonely noise—the sound of others' pleasure.

Patricia tugged at my shirt. "Let's join in."

"I'm feeling queasy," I said. "I'm not used to the . . . motion."

"Where are you going?"

I hurried through the rooms, corridors, and decks of the boat, looking for somewhere she wouldn't find me for a while. For ages I heard her calling my name.

I found a small cabin. Candles were burning; the music was North African. There were oriental cushions, wall hangings, rugs, a lot of velvet. The style amused me, reminding me of the 1960s.

I liked the boat. Why couldn't I get work as a deckhand? But I was annoyed at having to leave the Center, where I had expected to spend the rest of my time in this body. But I had got in too far with the people there. It was no longer restful. Whatever happened tonight, I would leave the island in the morning, taking the first boat wherever it went. I would go to another island and find a job in a bar or disco.

I heard footsteps. It wasn't Patricia, but Matte, the owner of the yacht, in shorts, bright shirt, and flip-flops.

"What the fuck are you doing in here?"

"Am I in the wrong place?" I got up. "You forgot to set aside a quiet room. It was chaotic and I needed to get away."

He walked right up to me and stared into my eyes. "Always ask first."

I said, "If I had a room, it'd be like this. The mid-sixties has always been one of my favorite periods."

"Right. Want a glass of wine now?"

"If that's okay. We were introduced, but in case you've forgotten, the name's Leo."

He said, "Matte. Why would someone your age be interested in the sixties?"

"Must be something to do with my parents. And you?"

He was fixing drinks for both of us. "Those days people knew how to have a laugh. 'Cept I was the wrong age."

His manner of speaking gave me the impression that English wasn't his first language, but it was impossible to tell where he was from. I'd have been inclined to say, if asked, "from nowhere."

"Was this your father's boat?"

His body stiffened. "Why the hell should it be?"

"I'm asking, is it a family possession?"

He said, "I hate it when people suggest I haven't worked, that I'm only a rich playboy. I do play at things—I play at being a playboy—but it's a vacation, not a vocation."

"Sorry," I said. "You wouldn't be the first to think of me as a fool. I'll get out."

He came after me and pulled me back roughly. "Wait right here. You have to stay now."

"Why?"

"I recognize you from somewhere."

"How could we have met? I'm neither a teacher nor student, only a cleaner at the Center on the island."

"Ever been a builder?"

"No."

"Coach driver?"

"Nope."

"I have seen you," he continued, screwing up his eyes. "It's not your face that I particularly recognize." He walked around me then, as if I were a sculpture. "It'll come back to me."

"Are you sure?"

"I might look like a hairy idiot but I've got perfect vision and an excellent memory."

He was making me nervous, more nervous, even, than Patricia. He chopped out some generous lines of coke and offered me one.

"Thanks," I said.

He was snorting one himself when there was a knock on the door. It was one of his Thai staff. Matte went to him and then, to my surprise, turned to me.

"I'm being told that someone called Patricia is looking for you."

"Oh, Christ."

Matte laughed, and said to the man, "He can't be found anywhere at the moment. He's indisposed." He shut the door. "She's after you, eh? Wants your body."

"Maybe I should appreciate her appreciation more. There'll be a time when no one will want to jump my old bones."

"The one thing I've never wanted is to get old, to see your own skin blotted and withered."

"Why is that?"

"I'm from a big family. As a kid, I hated grandmothers, aunts, old men and women kissing me. Their lips, mouths, breath over me—makes me nearly lose me lunch to think of it."

I said, "I remember my grandmother's cheeks and hands,

her cardigan, her smell, with nothing but love. She had learned things, which made me feel safe. Anyhow, you haven't been old yet. How do you know you won't like it?"

"I haven't died yet. Or visited Northampton. I just know they won't agree with me."

He kept looking at me as though there was something he wanted to know or ask me.

I said, "I'll only be here a minute. All I want to do is relax."

"You do that. I've got a party to run."

"Right."

Somewhat self-consciously, I turned to look out at the dark sea, hoping that when I turned back he'd be gone. I heard him lock the door. Before I could speak, I was hit, and lost my bearings.

Instinctively, I imagined Matte had struck me from behind, smashing his fist onto the back of my head with some strength. That was how it felt. But he had encircled my neck with his arm, kicked my legs away, and forced me to my knees. I thought: Now he's going to shoot me in the back of the head. During this I recalled, incorrectly I hope, a line from Webster: "Of all the deaths, a violent one is best."

"What are you doing?"

"Leo, shut it! If you keep still I won't damage you."

"Keep still for what?"

He was searching in my hair, not unlike the way I would grab my kids and examine their heads for nits. I said, "I never had you down for a madman."

"'Scuse me," he said, relaxing his grip. "I found the mark."

"Mark?"

"Didn't you know? I guess they like to believe it's all seamless. You can get up now. How old are you really? No need to pretend. I am nearly eighty. A good age in a man, don't you think?"

I murmured, "You look well."

"Thanks. So do you."

6

_____

HE SAID, *"Senex bis puer."*

"An old man is twice a boy?"

"That's the one. I've just taken up wrestling, along with the kickboxing." He put up his hands. "Wonderful sport. I'll show you a few moves later."

I wiped my face. "I think I've got the idea."

But I pushed him then, a couple of times, quickly, and he fell back. He was flushed with fury. For a moment, I thought we'd be wrestling. We'd have enjoyed that. But before he could react, I'd dropped my hands and was laughing, so the argument was whether he'd lose his temper or not.

He managed not to, distracting himself by opening a cabinet within which there was a monitor. He switched it on and flicked to a channel showing the orgy room. I spotted Alicia dancing alone, naked. She looked freer than I had seen her before.

"Want this on? Or would you prefer to slip into someone comfortable—when I've finished with you."

"Neither."

"Nor me," he said. "Nothing's ever new for people like us. It takes a lot to turn us on—if anything does at all."

"What else is there? Why have we done this?"

"But there is something left. You don't know?"

"Not unless you go to the trouble of telling me," I said.

"Murder. It is the deepest, loveliest thing. You haven't tried it yet?" I shook my head. "One must experience everything once, don't you think?"

I said, "No one's ever hit me like that."

"Shame."

"Why did you do it?"

He touched my neck, chest, and stomach. "I considered that body for myself, but wanted something a bit wider and more chunky. I'm surprised it hung around there for so long. Still, they did have an excellent choice of new facilities. It would have looked good on me. It doesn't look bad on you. How does it feel?"

I moved my limbs a bit. "Fine—until you attacked me."

"How long have you had it?"

"Not even three months."

"I didn't hurt you, did I?"

"I'll survive," I said. "I'm just a little annoyed. Thanks for the concern."

"It was your body I was thinking of, rather than you. Hey, what d'you think of my body?" Without waiting for a reply, he removed his shirt. "Sometimes, all you want is to be able to look in the mirror without disgust." I nodded approvingly, but, obviously, not approvingly enough. "What about this?" he said. He was showing me his penis, even slapping it against his leg with obscene pride. "It just goes on and on."

"Incomparable."

"That's what they all say. How are my buns?"

"Jesus. With those you could be your own hotdog."

"I've been in this body for three years. You get used to bodies, and the person you become in them. As with jeans, Newbodies are better the more they're worn in. You forget you're in them." He pulled at his stomach. "Look at that: I'm increasing here, but I don't want to be perfect. I figured out that perfection makes people crazy, or feel inferior."

"Whereas," I said, "it's one's weaknesses that people want to know?"

"Maybe," he said. "No one ever gets rid of those. I think I'll do another ten years—or even longer, if things go well—in this facility before moving on to something fitter." He filled his glass once more and held it out. "To us—pioneers of the new frontier!"

"We have a secret in common," I said, "you and me. Do you get to discuss it much with others?"

"They do talk about it, the 'newies.' But I want to live, not chatter. I love being a funky, dirty young man. I love pouting my sexy lips and being outstanding at tennis. My serve could knock your face off! You should have seen me before. I've got the photographs somewhere. What's the point of being rich if you're lopsided and have a harelip? It was a joke, a mistake that I came out alive like that! This is the real me!"

"What I miss," I said, "is giving people the pleasure of knowing about me."

He was unstoppable. "Soon everyone'll be talking 'bout this. There'll be a new class, an elite, a superclass of super-bodies. Then there'll be shops where you go to buy the body you want. I'll open one myself with real bodies rather than mannequins in the window. Bingo! Who d'you want to be today!"

I said, "If the idea of death itself is dying, all the meanings, the values of Western civilization since the Greeks, have changed. We seem to have replaced ethics with aesthetics."

"Bring on the new meanings! You're a conservative, then."

"I didn't think so. I guess I don't know what or who I am. It's always uplifting, though, to meet a hedonist—someone relieved of the tiring standards that hold the rest of us back from the eternal party."

"You still think I'm just a playboy, do you? Look at those books!" He pointed at a shelf. "I'm taking those in! Euripides, Goethe, Nietzsche. I'm dealing with the deepest imponder-ables. You know what happened to me? I was seventy-five years old. My wife leaves me—not for some virile fucker, but to become a Buddhist. She prefers old fat stomach to me! Some other cultures go for different body shapes, you know." He went on, "Mostly, my children don't bother with me. They're too busy with drugs! My friends are dead. I can buy women, but they don't desire me. I didn't just work all my life, I fought and scrambled and dug into the rock surface of the world with my fuckin' fingernails! I lost it all and I was dying and I was depressed. You think I wanted to check out in that state?"

"It sounds hard to say it, but that's a life, I guess. It's the failures, the hopeless digressions, the mistakes, the waste that add up to a lived life."

If he'd been in a pub, he'd have spat on the floor. "You're only an intellectual," he said. "I deserved a better final curtain. I bought one! I can tell you, I'm doing some other pretty worthwhile things. Let's hear from you now. What are you doing with your new time?"

"Me? I'm only a menial at the Center."

He made a face. "You're going to keep doing that?"

"I'm definitely not doing anything worthwhile. In fact, I can't tell you what a relief it is to have had a career rather than having to make one. Now I'm going to enjoy my six months."

"You're really going back into your slack old bodysuit?"

"This is an experiment. I wanted to find out what this would be like. But I'm still afraid of anything too . . . unnatural."

He had been pacing about. Now he sat down opposite me. His tone was more than businesslike; he was firm, but not quite threatening, though it seemed he could become so.

He said, "You can sell that one, then."

"Sell what?"

"That body."

"Sell it?"

"Yeah, to me. I'll pay you well. You will make a substantial profit which you and your family can live on for the rest of your God-given life."

"What about my old body?"

"I'll get that back for you. No problem. An old body sack is about as valuable as a used condom." He was looking at me passionately. "It's a good deal. What do you say?"

"I'm puzzled. You've got the money. Go and buy one. I went to a place, a kind of small hospital. I'm sure you did the same."

"I did. You think those places are easy to find? It's not that simple anymore."

"What d'you mean?"

"You were either well connected or lucky," he said. He was drumming his fingers. "Things have changed already."

"In what way?" He didn't want to say. "To put it objectively," I went on, "if people want bodies so badly, they could eliminate someone. Unlike you, I'm not recommending it, only suggesting what seems obvious. This isn't the only desirable body around."

"Bodies have to be adapted. The 'mark' on the head tells you that's been achieved. The body you are in now isn't valuable in itself, but the work that's been done on it is. The people who do it are like gods, extending life. There are only three or four doctors in the world today who can do this operation, and they're like the men who made the atomic bomb—hated, admired, and feared, having changed the nature of human life."

"Do you know these body artists?"

"I can get to at least one of them," he said. "And I have ill acquaintances who will pay a great deal to be moved into another body facility."

"People who will give everything rather than die. I can understand that. Wow, I'm in big demand," I said. "But I'll wait for my six months to be up. What's the rush?"

"Someone might be dying in awful pain with only weeks to live. They might not be able to wait for your little 'tryout' to come to an end."

"That, as they say, is life."

"What the fuck are you talking about?"

I said, "Is it someone you know? A friend or a lover?"

"Shut up!"

I said, "Fine. But that's what I've decided to do. I'm not handing my body over to anyone. I'm just settling in. We're getting attached."

"But you don't even want it! How can a few months matter when you're going back? I would advise you most strongly to sell it now."

"Strongly, eh?"

"If I were you, I wouldn't want to put myself in unnecessary danger. You're not the sort to be able to look after yourself."

"Matte, it's my decision. I don't want your money, and I don't want my 'body holiday' interrupted."

He was having difficulty controlling himself. Some anxiety or fury was flooding him. He walked about the cabin, with his face turned away from me.

"The demand is there," he said. "The bodies of young women, on which there has always been a premium, are in big demand in the United States. These women are disappearing from the streets, not to be robbed or raped but to be painlessly murdered. There are machines for doing it, which I am hoping to be involved in the manufacture of. It's a beautiful procedure, Leo. The sacked bodies are kept in fridges, waiting for the time when the operation will have been simplified. When it'll be like slotting an engine into a car, rather than having to redesign the car itself each time. People might even start to share bodies to go out in, the way girls share clothes now. They'll say to one another, 'Who'll wear the body tonight?' There's no going back. Immortality is where some of us are heading, like it or not. But there will be some people for whom it will be too late."

I was interested to meet someone in my situation and I

would have liked to have spent at least one evening with a group of Newbodies—we waxen immortals—sitting around a card table, discussing the past, of which there would have been plenty, no doubt. His tone concerned me, however. I was afraid and wanted to get out of there but he had locked the door. I didn't want to provoke him; he seemed capable of anything. So when he said, "Come, look at this—it might interest you," I went with him.

I followed him through narrow, twisting corridors. We passed a door outside of which stood two big men in white short-sleeved shirts. Matte nodded at the men and exchanged a few words with one of them in Greek. I was going to ask Matte what they were guarding, but I had been too curious already.

We went down another corridor. At last, Matte knocked on the door of another cabin. An upper-class English voice said, "Come."

The room was dark, apart from the light shed by a table lamp. At a desk sat a woman in her thirties, writing and listening to gentle big-band music. Her clothes appeared to be from another time, my mother's, perhaps, though I could see her hair and teeth were not. If there was something palpably strange about her, I'd have said she resembled an actress in a period film whose contemporary health and look belied the period she appeared to be representing.

Matte went to her. They spoke, and she continued her work.

He stood beside me at the door and whispered, "That woman is a child psychologist, a genius in her field. Years ago, as a man, she looked after one of my children who was seriously disturbed. She knows almost everything about human beings. When he was ill, not long ago, I paid for him to become a Newbody. He had arthritis and was bent double. He needed to finish his book and to continue to help others, as a woman. Don't you think that's a pretty charitable thing?" He gave me a look that was supposed to shame me. "She's not sweeping the floor somewhere and chasing sex." He shut the door. "What would you ask her?"

"How to die, I guess."

"Death is dead."

"Oh, no, everyone'll miss it so, and there would be other psychologists," I said, "to build on his or her work."

"She can do that herself. Life renewing itself."

"How's her book?"

"Looks like she'll need several lifetimes. She's . . . thorough."

"Read it?"

"A boxful of notes? Most of the time she lies on deck, 'thinking.' She has too much sex for my liking. I'll accept one of your points: she'd go faster if she thought she was going to snuff it. Wish she'd update her taste, too. She insists on listening to that old-time music, which reminds me of days I want to forget."

"I guess you can't force anyone to like speed garage," I said. "Do your kids know you now?"

"They don't know where I am. They're not speaking to me. When they get older, if they behave themselves, I'll get them new bodies as birthday presents."

"They'll want that?"

"Those crazy kids'll totally love it. They've been in bands and clinics and stuff. They get exhausted—you know, the lifestyle. This way they can carry on. I'm holding off telling them because I know they're gonna want to get off to a new start right away."

"What's wrong with that?"

"If they haven't suffered enough, they're not gonna appreciate it. This isn't for everybody."

I didn't want to listen to him, or argue anymore. As with Ralph Hamlet, I found the encounter disturbing. Matte and I were both mutants, freaks, human unhumans—a fact I could at least forget when I was with real people, those with death in them.

I said, "I need to see where Patricia is."

For a moment I thought he wouldn't let me go. But what could he do? He was thinking hard, though. Then we shook hands. "There's plenty of women here who would be attracted to you," he said. "Take who you want."

"Thanks."

"You must think more seriously about the body sale." He gave me his card and looked me up and down once more. "I'm your man—first in line with a bag of cash. Look after yourself."

I knew he was watching me walk away.

I went outside. The moon and stars were bright; the air was warm. On the deck, most of the guests had gathered and were dancing wildly, yelling and whistling. The female Newbody I'd met earlier was performing: kicking out, swaying and singing in front of a guitarist and keyboard player, encouraging us to worship her as she worshipped herself.

I asked someone, "What's she called?"

"Miss Reborn," I was told.

When I touched Patricia on the shoulder, she took me in her arms. "I looked for you everywhere."

"Matte and I were talking."

"He wanted your opinion on things, eh?" she said with unnecessary sarcasm.

"I can't say I learned a lot about him."

"Why not?" she said. "Up here, I've been following the rumors and fantasies. His family are wealthy, that's for sure."

"Is that all?"

"Kiss me." I did so. She said, "His beloved brother, who is much older than him, is dying, apparently, from an incurable disease."

"His brother?"

"Dying painfully—on this boat, in a sealed cabin, they say."

"Really?"

"He is yards from us, as we frolic here." I recalled the two men guarding a door. "That's made you think."

"Why don't we dance while there's time? I can't believe that singer. Look at her move."

"Oh, yes," she said. "Why didn't you suggest we dance earlier?"

"It's not too late."

"You little liar, you weren't talking to Matte at all," she said. "You were fucking. You're all cock. How many were there?"

"Too many to mention."

"I know that if you and I are to be together it's something I'm going to have to live with."

"That's right."

Her head was on my shoulder. While we danced, I could think over what Matte had said. It wasn't difficult to see why he wanted my body for his brother. But why didn't he go and buy one, as I had? That was what I didn't understand—why he was so keen on me.

I tried to forget about it. I began to enjoy dancing with Patricia, holding and kissing her, examining the folds and creases of her old neck and full arms, the excess flesh of her living body, and holding her mottled hands. I thought about something he'd said, "Who wants a lot of Oldbodies hanging about the world? They're ugly and expensive to maintain. Soon, they'll be irrelevant."

Yet there was something in her I didn't want to let go of. Her body and soul were one, she was "real," but how could such a notion count against immortality?

Matte had filled me with anxiety and foreboding. I wasn't aware of how long Patricia and I danced, but I guessed the night was gone. We must have been around the islands and back to where we'd started. I'd been on that boat far too long.

Patricia had her hands inside my shirt. "You make me feel all slippy. I want you again. I can't wait to have you."

Much as I was glad to be with her, I didn't think I could go through all that.

"You might have to wait a bit," I said.

"Why?"

"Oh, I don't know. I'm tired. Look," I said. "There's plenty of men about. Young men on their own, too."

I could see at least three or four well-built guys standing around the edge of the dance floor.

"Tell me something," she said. I noticed a new clarity in her eyes. "You won't tell me the truth, I know that. But I'll know anyway. Does touching me, kissing me, licking me . . . is it something you'd rather not do? Does my body disgust you?"

Her physical presence, her body, didn't repel me, in fact. My sister had been a nurse. She'd taught me not to find bodies repellent, only the people inside them. It was Patricia's proprietorial attitude I found difficult. While I was thinking about this, she watched me.

"Now I know," she said. "I thought that was it. It took me a while to figure it out."

"Yes," I said. "What you do to me is a description of what you say men do to women, lower and humiliate them. It's fascistic. Patricia, whatever happened to the revolution?"

She stepped back from me, as if something had exploded inside her body.

I slipped away, moving quickly now. It wasn't her I wanted to get away from. Out of the corner of my eye I had seen Matte pointing me out to another man, who was looking to see where I was. Other men were moving toward him.

I went around to the other side of the yacht and stripped off to my pants. I tied my shoes together and stuck them down the back. I could see a few lights on the shore in the distance. Preparations were being made for disembarkation, but it would take some time. I couldn't wait. I climbed onto the rail and dived into the sea.

I had surfaced and been swimming a few minutes when I heard voices. There were splashes behind me. Others were joining in. Why? I stopped for a moment and looked behind. By the light of the ship, I could tell that the swimmers following me didn't resemble women from the Center, but men from the boat. They were not stoned or drunk revelers either. They were swimming with purpose, without churning up the water. They must have been Matte's men. They were quick and strong. So was I; and I had the advantage, just.

I ran out of the water, put on my shoes, and sprinted up the beach into the village. A few bars and discos were still open. The square was full of noise and people. I could have disappeared into the crowd somewhere, but what then? Soon everyone would start to disperse. Anyhow, I didn't want to risk running into any of my other enemies.

I hurried through the narrow alleys toward the Center. When I got there, it was deserted, to my relief. I relaxed a little and made myself a cup of tea. I would hide out in the place until the morning. But the more I thought about it, the less safe I felt. The men following me had seemed determined. It wouldn't have been difficult for Matte to find out where I was staying, and he was ruthless.

As I was collecting my washbag and a few other things from the roof, I thought I heard someone rattling the handle of the door in the wall. I didn't hear any raised female voices either. Hurrying now, I picked up several items of women's clothing, spread out on the roof to dry, and shoved them in my rucksack.

When I heard voices within the building and saw a torchlight flash, I leapt from the roof of the accommodation block to the roof of the kitchen. I jumped down the side of the building to a narrow concrete ledge below. I knew the only way out now was down the side of the hill. I wasn't sure how steep it was exactly, but I was in no doubt that it was a stiff gradient.

Not only that, the terrain was rough. As I teetered there, trying to decide what to do, I was aware of how strong the desire to live was. Had it come to it, I could have stood on that ledge for days. I'd been depressed in my life, at times; suicidal, even. But I wasn't ready to give up my mind or my body. I wanted to live.

I jumped. It must have been twenty feet down. After hitting the earth, every staggering step was perilous. It seemed to be rocky and sandy at the same time. I couldn't stop to think. I slipped and fell most of the way; it was impossible for me to stay on my feet. My body got cut all over. What was the foliage made of? Tin? Razors? It was like rolling through broken glass. However, to my knowledge I wasn't being followed.

At the bottom of the hill, I halted. I couldn't hear anyone following me. I waited for more of the night to pass. Cautiously, I made my way toward the beach. By now, even the copulators had gone.

I broke into the bathroom of a deserted restaurant, where I washed and shaved off my beard. Then I lay down on some benches, pulling a damp tarpaulin on top of me. There were slithery creatures, insects and dogs around, and men who wanted my body. I didn't sleep.

I was at the harbor before it was light, waiting for the first boat to take me back to Piraeus. I'd get to Athens and decide my next move. I had covered my head in a long, light scarf; I wore a wraparound skirt and dark glasses. I wouldn't get on the boat until the last moment.

I was sitting at the back of a café facing the harbor when someone whispered the name I'd so foolishly given myself in my arrogance. Even as I thought of running once more, I began to shiver with terror.

Alicia, of course, had come looking for me.

"How did you find me?" I said. I indicated my outfit. "Do these colors suit me?"

"Yes, but not all at once."

"Some of the men on the island have been threatening me again. I know they work down here."

She said, "I thought: What would I do here? Where would I hide? And there you were."

"Right," I said. "Do I look conspicuous?"

"Only to me. Anyone try to pick you up yet?"

"I'm too much of a tragic figure."

"A tragic figure with most unladylike hairy ears," she said. We had coffee together. She said, "You're running."

"Time to move on. Did you enjoy it last night?"

"Something strange happened. I'll tell you about it another time." Then she said, "I won't be staying at the Center much longer. Patricia will be after me, when she finds you've gone. I'm disappointed you're fleeing like this."

"I'm sorry if I have made things difficult for you, but she'll never leave me alone."

"It's the price the beautiful have to pay. Aren't you used to it yet?"

Watching the boat being loaded up, I was getting nervous; I asked if she minded getting me a ticket from the harbor office. I could see several likely candidates for Matte's men.

On the ship, I hid in the women's toilet. After, when people started to bang on the door, I had to come out. I thought I was done for. I made my way to the car deck and hid under a blanket on the backseat of an old Mercedes. The boat docked and the driver got in without noticing me. Outside, as the traffic queued to leave, I hopped out of the car and ran for it. I sprinted out of there and into the crowd, and got a taxi.

7
———

I'm not sure why, but I returned to the part of London I knew. I felt safer, and more at ease in my mind, in a familiar place. In your own city, you don't have to think about where you are. Being pursued had frightened me; I was scared all the time now. I had no idea whether Matte would still be following me. I must have convinced myself that he'd lost interest in me. Perhaps his brother had died; maybe he'd found another body. I am, however, old enough to know how few of our thoughts bear any relation to the way things are.

I checked into the same dismal hotel as before. When I needed money I worked in a factory packing Christmas toys. Perhaps Matte was right, and it had been a mistake to "hire" a body for six months. I didn't have time to begin a new life as a new person, and, expecting to go back, I missed my old life. I was in limbo, a waiting room in which there was no reality but plenty of anxiety.

One morning at eight, there was a knock on my door.

In this hotel, there were always knocks on the door— refugees, thieves, prostitutes, drug dealers; people who would never be able to afford new bodies or even to feed adequately the one they already had; people looking for other people and no one wanting to do you a favor, if it wasn't in exchange for another one. Usually, though, they would declare themselves. This time there was no reply.

Maybe Matte had come for my body. I'd seen the movie. Men in dark suits were outside. While they were kicking the door in, I'd hide in the shower with my gun, or climb out of the bathroom window and down the fire escape. That was the young man's route, and I wouldn't be a young man in my mind, however lithe my body. For there was another part of me, my older mind, if you like, which was, by now, outraged by the violation, the cheek of it. My body wasn't for sale, though I had, of course, purchased it myself.

"How did you find me?"

Alicia was sitting on the bed; I stood looking at her. She had shaved her head and put on weight. She wore a top with a bow at the front.

"Why have you grown a full beard?"

"Alicia, I am hoping to be taken seriously."

I'd forgotten how nervous she was. "Leo, it's good to see you. How much do you mind me coming to see you?"

"Not as much as you might think. I do need to know how you tracked me down."

"I haven't told Patricia—she isn't downstairs, if that's what's bothering you. I looked through your things one time . . . trying to . . . I wanted to know who you were. You do know, I guess, that you're as elusive as a spy. It turned me into a spy. I found a receipt for this hotel and wrote the address into one of my poems. Still," she said, "if you want to be private, why shouldn't you be? Do you want me to go?"

"I'll come with you. Let's get out of here. I never stay in this room during the day."

I was putting on my coat.

She said, "You're writing."

In the corner of the room, on a small table, were some papers.

"Please don't look at that," I said.

"Why not?"

"Leave it! I'm trying . . . to do something about an old man in a young man's body."

"You've done a lot. Is it a film?" She was turning the pages. "There's dialogue. It's professionally laid out. Have you written before?"

"You encouraged me, Alicia."

"It was the other way around. Will you try to sell it?"

"You never know. Give it here now."

"What a strange boy you are!"

I took the papers from her and put them under the bed.

In the café, I asked, "How is my friend Patricia?"

"What a troublemaker you are. People had paid to attend her classes but she refused to get out of bed. You showed her something was possible, some intensity of feeling with a man, and you took it away again. She would send for me and we'd talk about you for hours, wondering who you were. She would rage and weep. The only relief was when that man from the boat came to see her."

"Man?"

"The playboy. Matte."

"Alicia, what happened?"

"I was sent out of the room. I heard everything from outside the window."

"And?"

"You owed him something, he said. He wouldn't say what it was. You didn't borrow money from him?" I shook my head. "He wanted to find you, wanted to know whether there was anyone who knew you."

"Did he threaten Patricia?"

"He didn't need to. She was delighted to talk about the intricacies of your character, insofar as she understood it, for hours. Not that this interested Matte. Of course, she doesn't know where you are. I left the island a few days later and went to Athens."

"Were you followed?"

"Why would I be? What's going on?" Alicia said. "You know what Patricia wanted? For you to run the place with her."

"I'd have liked to do that," I said. "For a while. It would have been fun. Impossible, too, of course, with her attitude toward me."

"You'd have done it?" she said. "Don't you have any doubts?"

"What?"

"About yourself. About what you are capable of? That makes you different to a lot of people. Different to most people, in fact."

"Yes," I said, "I do have doubts. I just don't want them getting in the way of my mistakes."

She said, "Something else happened. I haven't told you the whole story. When you disappeared from the boat that last night—"

"Yes, sorry. I couldn't stand it—"

"Some people went back to the Center. But I was hanging around to see whether you might return. A lot of our group stayed on the boat until after breakfast. The dawn was lovely. Matte came to me. He realized I was from the Center. I don't look like the other people he knows, with their perfect bodies. He took me to his room. He wanted information about you."

"What did you say?"

"He was sitting there opposite me, opening and shutting his legs like a trap. He looked almost as handsome as you. I promised to tell him everything I knew about you if he fucked me. I told him I was an unorgasmic virgin. It was time, you see. He was amused, and seems to have looked into these things. 'Apparently, the use of virgins,' he told me, 'prolongs life. The headmaster of a Roman school for girls lived to one hundred and fifty. Rather that than ingesting the dried cells of fetal pigs, or drinking snake oil.' He seemed to think it was a decent exchange. He fucked me hard, right there on the floor. It was wonderful. Is it always like that? I'm pregnant."

"By him? Matte?"

She patted her stomach. "Don't ask me if I'll keep it."

"The world is full of single mothers. It's the only way, these days. What use are men? But he's not a good man."

"I don't need to tell you, a good man is hard to find. Ask Patricia!"

"Alicia, that was a mad thing to do! You don't know him!"

"One day, I'll present him with a bill."

"But why him?"

"You'd turned me on and I couldn't wait any longer. No one else on that boat seemed much interested in having me. I know I'm not beautiful, and as a girl all I wanted was to be beautiful. Matte was looking at me like a hungry wolf I couldn't keep from the door."

"It's like having a kid with the devil."

"If he's really bad, you'd better tell me the details. I can only consider my position if I know the facts. Otherwise . . . I'm going ahead with it."

She was waiting; she seemed to be aware that there was more I knew.

"I only met him once," I said. I kissed and cuddled her. "Congratulations."

"Thanks."

"What will you do now?"

"I'm back living with Mother. Things are dark. I need to tell you, I don't know how to go on."

I was looking at her. "People either want eternal life or they want out right now."

"Can you think of reasons to continue?"

"Lots. Pleasure."

"Only that?"

"Children," I added, "if you like them. They always gave me more pleasure than anything else."

"Good, good," she said.

With her, I always felt I had to justify the most basic things, which discomforted me. Still, I liked her; I'd always liked her. I wanted to help her. Then I had an idea. I told her I had something to sort out; we agreed to meet later.

When we parted, I went to an Internet café and sent an email in my given name, to a friend who was the editor of a literary magazine that published fiction, some journalism, and photographs. I urged him to see Alicia as soon as possible. I told him I didn't want my name mentioned. Then I rang Alicia and told her she had to go and see this man after lunch. After some argument she agreed to go to his office, read him a couple of poems, and talk about herself.

Later that day, when we met again in a local pub, she told me he'd given her a job reading manuscripts and sorting out the office three days a week.

"That's great," I said. "Are you pleased?"

She kissed me. "I knew that somehow this had happened through you, Leo. But the odd thing was, he didn't know your name."

"No," I said. "He wouldn't remember me. But my father was well connected."

"Who was your father? Or is that your privacy, right?"

We were sitting in a bar by the window where I could monitor the street for murderers. I recognized a few local people. They all looked like murderers. However, there was one person in particular I had been looking out for during the last few days, without properly admitting it to myself, someone I couldn't search out, but had to wait for.

It had to be now. There she was, my wife, across the road. The wheel of her shopping cart had come off. She was fiddling with it, but it would have to be fixed properly. At a loss, she stood there, looking around. The cart was heavy, full of provisions. She couldn't leave it and she couldn't carry it home.

I asked Alicia to excuse me. I crossed the road to my wife and asked if she was okay.

"I'm rather stuck, dear."

"These small accidents can be devastating. Can I?"

I hauled the cart into a doorway and took a look at it. I'm not mechanical, but I could see the wheel had sheared off.

"Do you live far?"

"Ten minutes' walk."

I said, "I'll be a good Samaritan. Wait one minute."

I went back to Alicia.

"This is my good deed for the week, perhaps for the century. Meet me in three hours at the pub on the corner."

She was looking at me. "You'd go home with any woman, apart from me."

"It must seem like that."

"Can't we bring up the kid together?"

I kissed her. "Later."

I recrossed the road and picked up the cart in my arms.

"Which way?"

It was heavy and awkward. I walked slowly, with exaggerated complaints, in order to spend more time with my wife.

"Don't you have anyone to help you?" I said.

"Not at the moment."

We were approaching my house. I noticed the front gate was wonky and needed repairing.

She opened the front door. "Would you like to come in?" I hesitated. "Just for a minute," she said.

"If it's all right with you. I wouldn't mind a glass of water."

Inside, she said, "Can I ask . . . what do you do?"

"I've been traveling. Gap year."

She went into the kitchen and I looked around. Nothing had changed, but everything was slightly different.

My son, now the same age as me, came downstairs and put his head around the door. I almost gave way. It was him I wanted to touch, his hands and face. In the last few years it had become more difficult for us to touch each other. He was embarrassed, or he didn't like my body. I loved, still, to kiss his cheeks, even if I had to grab him and pull him toward me.

"All right, Mum?" Mike said. "Hello," he said to me.

I must have been staring.

"My cart broke," she said.

"Your heart?" he said.

"Cart, you big idiot!"

He came into the room. He looked alert, happy, and healthy. I could see my old self in the way he held himself. I missed me. I missed, too, my pleasure in him, in living close to his life, in knowing what he did and where he went.

I was dismayed to see he was carrying my new laptop, a gorgeous little sliver of light I'd bought just before deciding to become someone else. I had been intending to use it in bed. I had always been attracted to the instruments of my trade. Sometimes, merely buying a new pen or computer was enough to get me back to work.

"That looks good," I said.

"Yes." He said to his mother, "I'm borrowing this for a while. I'll return it before Dad gets back. Have you heard from him?"

"He sent his love," she called.

"Is that all?" he said. "He won't mind me borrowing this, then. By the way, happy anniversary. Shame to be on your own."

"I'll raise a glass later," she said.

I said, "Can I ask what anniversary it is?"

"Not my wedding anniversary," she said, "but the anniversary of the day I met my husband. He's away on business at the moment, the fool."

"Why fool?"

"His breathing was painful. He couldn't walk far. I could see it in his face, but I don't think he knew how ill he had become. Before he started out on his jaunt across the continent, I had decided we should enjoy the time we had left together. Still, I didn't want to put him off his pleasures."

Mike said, "Mum, are you okay? Can I go?"

"Please do."

He shut the front door.

I asked, "Would you like me to get going, too?"

"But I must offer you some tea. I'd feel bad if I didn't, after you helped me."

"You're very trusting."

"I noticed you looking at the books just now. No burglar or lunatic would do that."

"Your boy is a great-looking kid."

"He's doing well. His girlfriend's pregnant."

"Really? How wonderful. Congratulations."

"Adam will be back for the birth, I know he will."

I went upstairs to the bathroom. Coming out, I noticed my study door was open. The books I'd been using before I left were piled on the coffee table, next to the CDs I'd bought but not yet played. I couldn't resist sitting down at my desk. I looked at the photographs of my children at various ages. I knew where everything was, though my hands were bigger and my arms longer than before. The ink in my favorite fountain pen still flowed. I wrote a few words and shoved the paper in my pocket. I had to tear myself away.

When I returned, I sat beside Margot and poured the tea. I glanced at the wedding ring I'd bought her and said, "Where are you from?"

"Me? You're asking me?" she said. "Do you want to know?"

"Why not?"

"No one's much interested in women of my age."

When she told me where she was born, and a little about her parents, I asked other questions about her early life and upbringing. I followed what occurred to me, listening and prompting.

I had heard some of this before, in the years when we were getting to know each other. I had not, though, asked her about it for a long time. How many times can you have the "same" conversation? But the past was no more inert than the present: there were different tones, angles, details. She mentioned people I'd never heard of; she talked about a lover she'd cared for more than she'd previously admitted.

Her story made more sense to me now, or I was able to let more of it in. We drank tea and wine. She was stimulated by my interest, and amazed by how much there was to tell. She wanted to speak; I wanted to listen.

I asked only about her life before she met me. When my name arose and she did speak about me a little, I didn't follow it up. I wish I'd had the guts to listen to every word—my life judged by my wife, a summing-up. But it would have disturbed me too much.

How she moved me! Listening to her didn't tell me why I

loved her, only that I did love her. I wanted to offer her all that I'd neglected to give in the past few years. How withdrawn and insulated I'd been! It would be different when I returned as myself.

Two hours passed. At last, I said, "Now I really must get going. I should let you get on."

"What about you?" she said. She was shaking her head. "I feel as though I'm coming round from a dream. What have we been doing together?"

I went over to the table on which sat a stereo system and a pile of CDs.

"Can I play a tune?"

She said, "Oh, tell me, why did you ask me all those questions?"

"Did they bother you?"

"No, the opposite. They stimulated me . . . they made me think . . ."

"I'm interested in the past. I am thinking of becoming a medieval historian."

"Oh. Very good." She added, "But what you asked was personal, not historical. You are a curious young man, indeed."

"Something happened to me," I said. "I was changed by something. I . . ."

She waited for me to continue, but I stopped myself. Sometimes there's nothing worse than a secret, sometimes there's nothing worse than the truth.

She said, "What happened?"

"No. My girlfriend is waiting for me down the street."

I put on my wife's favorite record. I kissed her hands and felt her body against mine as we danced. I knew where to put my hands. In my mind, her shape fitted mine. I didn't want it to end. Her face was eternity enough for me. Her lips brushed mine and her breath went into my body. For a second, I kissed her. Her eyes followed mine, but I could not look at her. If I was surprised by the seducibility of my wife, I was also shocked by how forgettable, or how disposable, I seemed to be. For years, as children, our parents have us believe they could not live without us. This necessity, however, never applies in the same way again, though perhaps we cannot stop looking for it.

At the door, my wife said, "Will you come for tea again?"

"I know where you are," I replied. "I don't see why not."

"We could go to an exhibition."

"Yes."

I said goodbye and reluctantly left my own house. Margot had placed a bag of rubbish outside the front door, ready to be taken to the dustbins. I was annoyed my boy hadn't done it; he must have had his hands full, carrying my laptop.

I took the rubbish around to the side of the house. From where I stood, through a hole in the fence, I could see the street. There was a car double-parked on the other side of the road, with two men in it. It was a narrow street and irritable drivers were backed up behind the car. Why didn't they move on? Because the men in the car were watching the house.

I slipped out of the front gate and headed up the road, away from them. It was true: they were following me. I went into my usual paper shop. Outside, the men were waiting in the car. When I continued on my way, they followed me. Who were these men who followed other men?

I knew the streets. Under the railway line, beside the bus

garage, was a narrow alleyway through which, years ago, I'd walked the children to school. I turned into it and ran; they couldn't follow me in the car.

Of course, they wanted me badly and were waiting at the top of the alley. This wasn't the death I wanted. I walked quickly. Farther down the street the three of them got out of the car and stood around me. Their faces were close; I could smell their aftershave. There were a lot of people on the street.

"Where are you taking me?"

"You'll find out."

Another of them murmured, "I've got a gun."

One of them had put his hand on my arm. It riled me; I don't like being held against my will. Yet I gained confidence; the gun, if it was really a gun, had helped me. I didn't believe they'd shoot me. The last thing they'd want to do was blow up my body.

I started to shout, "Help me! Help me!"

As people turned to look, the men tried to pull me into the car, but I kicked and hit out. I heard a police siren. One of the men panicked. People were looking. I was away, and running through the closely packed market stalls. The three of them weren't going to chase me with guns through the crowd on market day.

As soon as I could, I rang Ralph's mobile from a phone box.

It was impossible for us to meet. He was "up to his neck in literature." Unfortunately for him, the fool had already told me where he was.

Half an hour later, I pushed open the pub door and entered. I'm a sentimentalist and want always for there to be the quiet interminability of a London pub in the afternoon, rough men playing pool, others just sitting in near silence, smoking. I couldn't see Ralph, but did notice a sign that said "Theatre and Toilets." I tripped down some narrow stairs into an oppressive, dank-smelling room, painted black. There were old cinema seats and, in one corner, a box office the size of a cupboard. Pillars seemed to obstruct every clear view of the tiny stage. I saw from the posters that they were doing productions of *The Glass Menagerie* and *Dorian Gray*.

A woman hurried over, introducing herself as Florence O'Hara. She wanted to know how many tickets I wanted for *The Glass Menagerie*, in which she played the mother. Or did I want tickets for *Hamlet*, in which she played Gertrude? If I wanted to see them both, there was a special offer.

As she said this, I was surprised to see, sitting in the gloom, unshaven and in a big overcoat, a well-known actor, Robert Miles, who'd been in a film I'd written seven years ago. Before it began shooting, he and I had had tea together several times.

I looked at Florence more closely. I could recall Robert trying to get her a small part in the film. They'd been lovers, and were still connected in some way.

Had I not been inhabiting this wretched frame, Robert and I could, no doubt, have exchanged greetings and gossip. Instead, when he saw me looking at him, being both nervous and arrogant, he got up and walked out.

At the same time, Ralph emerged, in the costume of a Victorian gentleman or dandy, with a top hat in his hand. We shook hands, and I sat behind him in the theater seats.

"I haven't got long," he said.

"Nor me."

"There's a show later. During the day, I'm working on a new play with Robert Miles. He's trying his hand at directing. I'm working with the best now."

Ralph was looking tired; his face seemed a little more lined than before.

He said, "I'm playing Dorian Gray as well. Florence is Sybil. I'm having the time of my life here." He glanced at me. "What's wrong? What can I do for you now?"

I told Ralph that Matte had "recognized" me, was a New-body himself, required a body for his brother, and was in pursuit of mine. How could this not bother Ralph? After all, wasn't he, theoretically, in a similar position?

"You come to me with these problems, but what can I do about any of them?"

"Ralph, anyone would recognize that, as with anything uniquely valuable—gold, a Picasso—bad people will be scrambling and killing for it. How could they not? But I can't just remove this body as I could a necklace."

"At least, not yet," he said. Ralph was looking around agitatedly. "You stupid fool. Why have you come here? You might have led them to me. They could kidnap me while I'm onstage and strip me down to my brain."

"How would they know you're a freak like me?"

"Don't fucking call me a freak! Only if you bloody well tell them. And I'm always afraid my maturity is going to give me away. What have you done to alert these people?"

By now, I was yelling, and I had big lungs.

"If you think this isn't going to be something that a lot of people aren't going to know about, you're a fool."

He leaned closer to me. "You get full-on, full-time security.

Big guys around you all the time. That's the price of a big new dick and fresh liver."

"How am I going to afford it?"

"You'll have to work."

"At what?"

"What d'you think? You used to be a writer. You can start again, in another style. You could become . . . let's say, a magical realist!" I could see Florence in the dressing-room doorway, waving at him. "Imagine where I'll be in ten years' time, in fifteen, in twenty! How do you know I won't be running one of the great theaters or opera houses of the world?" I was sitting there with my head in my hands. "I didn't tell you. I will now. Ophelia and I—the girl playing that part, of course—are getting married. I didn't tell you this, either: we have a child together. A few days old, and perfect. I was afraid for a while that it would be some kind of oddity."

"Well done."

"Are you going to see the show? Maybe it's better you don't hang around here, if you're being chased."

I indicated my body. "All I want," I said, "is to be rid of this, to get out of this meat. I want to do it tonight, if possible." He was looking at me pityingly. "I guess I could find the hospital myself, but I'm in a hurry. What's the address of the place you took me to?"

"Up to you," he said, skeptically.

He told me the address. I wouldn't forget it. He was glad to be rid of me.

I said, "Good luck with the show. I'll come and see it in a few days' time, with my wife. She and I are planning to spend a lot of time together."

At the top of the stairs, I heard Florence's voice behind me. "What name?" she called.

"What?"

"What name for the tickets to the show?"

"I'll let you know."

"Don't you even know your own name?"

Coming into the pub was a young woman with a baby in a sling. Ralph's kid, I guessed. But I was in too much of a hurry to stop. There was a miserable cab office at the end of the street where, in my old frame, I had known the drivers and listened to their stories.

I told the cabbie to drive fast. As we went, I looked around continuously, staring into every car and face for potential murderers, thinking hard, convinced I was still being followed. Where I was going wasn't far, but I had to be careful.

Not long after we'd left the city, I said, suddenly, to the driver, "Drop me off here."

"I thought you wanted—"

"No, this is fine." We were approaching an area of low, recently built industrial buildings. "Listen," I said, holding up the last of my money, "give me the petrol can you keep in the back of the car. I've broken down nearby, and I'm in a hurry."

He agreed, and we went around to the boot of the car. He gave me the can and I wrapped it in a black plastic bag. I picked it up and headed for a pub I'd noticed. There, I had a couple of drinks and went into the toilet. I locked the cubicle door and stripped.

It took some time and I was careful and thorough. When I'd finished, and got back into my clothes, I left the pub and ran through the bleak streets toward the building, or "hospital," I remembered. Soon, I was disoriented, but the address was right. The layout of the streets and the other buildings was the same. Then I saw it. The place had changed. It could have been years ago that I was there. The building I believed to be the "hospital" was encircled by barbed wire; grass was poking up through the concrete. In the front, an abandoned filing cabinet was lying on its side. What sort of elaborate disguise was this?

I climbed the fence and pushed my way through the wire, which had been severed in several places. Nobody seemed bothered about security. The front door of the "hospital" wasn't even locked. However, it was getting dark. I tried the lights, but the electricity had been turned off. Bums had probably been sleeping there on rotten mattresses. The place also seemed to have been vandalized by local kids. I guessed that everything important had been taken away long before that. There were no bodies around, neither new nor old. I didn't know what to do now but there was no reason to stay.

I heard a voice.

8

"WE WEREN'T too bothered about capturing you earlier. We guessed you'd end up here."

Matte emerged from the gloom. A torch was shining in my face. I covered my eyes.

I asked, "You always knew about this place?"

"I knew the caravan would have moved on, but figured out you'd be less well connected than me. I still need that body."

"Looks like I'm going to need it myself."

"You've argued yourself out of it. Someone else's need is greater."

"Your brother?"

"What? Let me worry about him."

I said, "You can take the body. There's a lot of life still in it. All I want is the old one back."

"Come through here." He pointed to the door, and added, "This place smells bad, or is it just you?"

"It's the place, too."

He said, "Jesus, what the fuck have they been doing, burning bodies?"

I followed him, surrounded by his three men, into another room. I noticed there were no windows; the floors were concrete and covered with broken glass and other debris. The tiles had been pulled up and smashed. Long, bright neon lights were positioned precariously. A man in blue doctor's scrubs was standing there with two assistants, all of them masked. In the middle of the room stood the sort of temporary operating table they use on battlefields, along with medical instruments on steel trays. I was looking around for my old body. Maybe it was being kept in another room and they'd wheel it in. I couldn't wait to see it again, however crumpled or corpselike it might seem.

"Where's my old body?" I said to the man I assumed to be the doctor. "I won't get far without it."

He looked at Matte, but neither of them said anything.

"I see," I said. "There's no body. It's gone." I sighed. "What a waste."

"Tough luck," he said. "You're going to eternity. When I've sorted this out, my brother and I are off to Honolulu for a family reunion. The only shame is, he'll remind me of you."

I noticed, on the floor, what looked like a long freezer on its side. It was large enough for a body the size of mine. There was a wooden box, too, big enough for a dead brain. Brains didn't take up much room, I guessed, and were not difficult to dispose of.

"Can I have a cigarette?" I said.

"That's what did for my brother."

"My last," I said. "Then I'll give up. Promise."

"Glad to hear it," said Matte. "Okay. Get on with it."

One of the men handed me a cigarette. "Arsehole."

"You, too," I said.

The man made a move toward me. Matte said, "Don't damage him! No bruises, and don't cut him up."

I said, "I'm going to undress now, have a smoke, and then I'll be ready for you."

"Good boy," said Matte. "You wanted a death and now you're going to get one." When I removed my jacket and shirt, Matte looked at me approvingly. "You look good. You've kept yourself in shape."

"Look at my dick, guys." I was waving it at them. "Wouldn't you like to have one of these?"

Matte said, "What the fuck's that aftershave you're wearing?"

I lit my lighter, and moved backward.

"It's petrol," I said. "I'm soaked in it. Never had petrol in my hair before. You come near me, pal, and this body you want goes up in flames like a Christmas pudding. And you, too, of course."

I held the lighter close to my chest. I didn't know how much closer I could get it without turning into a bonfire. Still, rather self-immolation than the degradation that would otherwise be my fate. I'd go out with a bang, burning like a torch, screaming down the road.

Apart from Matte, everyone retreated. The doctors shrank back. Matte wanted to grab me. There was a moment when, to be honest, he could have done it. But the others' fear seemed to affect him. He didn't know what to do; all he could do was play for time.

There was nothing behind me but the door, which was open. I picked up my shirt and trousers before turning and fleeing. I ran, and I guess they ran, but I ran faster and I knew my way out of there.

I climbed the fence, got dressed, and continued to run. It was dark, but I was fit and had some idea where I was going. They'd get in their cars and pursue me, but I was being canny now. I was away. They would never find me.

It didn't occur to me for a long time to consider my destination. When I felt safe I rested in someone's garden. I needed a drink, but sweat and petrol don't smell good together. The last thing I needed was suspicious looks. I was carrying my credit cards, but I realized there was nowhere I could go now; not back to my wife, to my hotel, or to stay with friends. I wouldn't be safe until Matte's brother died, or Matte turned his attention elsewhere. Even then there could be other criminals pursuing me. It was as though I were wearing the *Mona Lisa*.

I was a stranger on the earth, a nobody with nothing, belonging nowhere, a body alone, condemned to begin again, in the nightmare of eternal life.

ABOUT THE AUTHOR

Hanif Kureishi was born and brought up in Kent. He read philosophy at King's College, London. In 1981 he won the George Devine Award for his plays *Outskirts* and *Borderline,* and in 1982 he was appointed Writer-in-Residence at the Royal Court Theatre. In 1984 he wrote *My Beautiful Laundrette,* which received an Oscar nomination for Best Screenplay. His second screenplay, *Sammy and Rosie Get Laid* (1987), was followed by *London Kills Me* (1991), which he also directed. *The Buddha of Suburbia* won the Whitbread Prize for Best First Novel in 1990 and was made into a four-part drama series by the BBC in 1993. His version of Brecht's *Mother Courage* has been produced by the Royal Shakespeare Company and the Royal National Theatre. His second novel, *The Black Album,* was published in 1995. With Jon Savage he edited *The Faber Book of Pop* (1995). His first collection of short stories, *Love in a Blue Time,* was published in 1997. His story "My Son the Fanatic," from that collection, was adapted for film and released in 1998. *Intimacy,* his third novel, was published in 1998, and a film of the same title, based on the novel and other stories by the author, was released in 2001 and won the Golden Bear award at the Berlin Film Festival. His play *Sleep With Me* premièred at the Royal National Theatre in 1999. His second collection of stories, *Midnight All Day,* was published in 2000. *Gabriel's Gift,* his fourth novel, was published in 2001. A film of his most recent script, *The Mother,* directed by Roger Michell, will be released in 2004. He has been awarded the Chevalier de l'Ordre des Arts et des Lettres.

M G 11/04

*

2/04

ML